A MIDSUMMER NIGHT'S DORK

OTHER NOVELS BY CAROL GORMAN

Carol Gorman

📖 HarperCollins*Publishers*

This one's for the Yoga Sisters:
Annie, Nina, and Robyn,
and for our guru, James

A Midsummer Night's Dork
Copyright © 2004 by Carol Gorman
Printed in the United States
of America. For information address HarperCollins Children's Books,
a division of HarperCollins Publishers,
1350 Avenue of the Americas, New York, NY 10019.
www.harperchildrens.com
Library of Congress Cataloging-in-Publication Data
Gorman, Carol.
A midsummer night's dork / Carol Gorman.—1st ed.
    p.   cm.
Summary: Jerry Flack, recently elected sixth-grade president, organizes an
Elizabethan festival at school but accepts a challenge from a bully that may
mean he will once again be considered a "dork."
    ISBN 0-06-050718-7 — ISBN 0-06-050719-5 (lib. bdg.)
    [1. Festivals—Fiction. 2. Popularity—Fiction. 3. Schools—Fiction. 4. Bullies—
Fiction.] I. Title.
PZ7.G6693Mg 2004   2003008213
[Fic]—dc21   CIP
                                                                AC
Typography by Hilary Zarycky
1   2   3   4   5   6   7   8   9   10
❖
First Edition

ACKNOWLEDGMENTS

My thanks to Michael Sokoloff, professional director and fight choreographer, for a fascinating session on stage fighting and for checking the stage-fighting scenes for accuracy.

Chapter One

Jerry Flack was late for school. He galloped along the sidewalk, his athletic shoes slapping a contrasting rhythm to his ragged gasps for air.

He had never been late to school in his whole life. *Only four minutes before the bell rings*, he thought. *Can't slow down till I hit the school grounds.*

The normal walk from home took a little over twelve minutes, provided that his pace was his usual three and a half miles per hour. He'd worked out the timing perfectly so that he'd always arrive ten minutes before the first bell. That way, he could hang out with his girlfriend, Brenda McAdams, for a while before they had to go inside.

But on this particular day, Jerry had overslept. A storm during the night had knocked out the electricity, and his clock radio hadn't gone off as it should have at 6:15 A.M. Instead, he awoke to his mother's screams that it was 7:52!

He'd leaped out of bed and pulled on his clothes. He'd grabbed a brush, and his hand was halfway to his head before he remembered that he didn't need to brush his hair. He'd run downstairs and grabbed the piece of buttered toast topped with strawberry jam that his mother held out to him on his way out the door. It felt like the relay races in PE when the runner behind passes the baton, and you take off, running your hardest, hoping that your slower-than-average speed won't cause your team to come in last.

Jerry arrived at school sweating, out of breath, with sticky fingers and two minutes to spare. He saw Brenda through the crowd, leaning against the tall oak near the door. It was their usual meeting place.

She spotted him and pushed off the tree. "Hey, Jerry. Did the storm knock out your electricity last night? I nearly called you to check."

"Yeah. I can't believe I overslept, today of all days."

Brenda grinned and flicked something off his face. "Crumb," she said. "Toast or something. Hey, your hair grew over the weekend. It'll be back to normal in no time."

"I hope so," Jerry said.

His hair was a lot shorter than normal, thanks to Gabe and Craig, two guys in his class who'd given him a custom cut on the floor of the boys' bathroom ten days ago. It had been a horrible experience, but Jerry was trying very hard to put it behind him. After all, a few minutes after that forced haircut, he'd been elected president of his sixth-grade class. Still, he was nervous about seeing those two guys today.

His heart was beating hard, and he knew it wasn't only because of his panicky run from home. He looked around him to make sure no one could hear. He lowered his voice. "You know, Gabe and Craig come back from suspension today."

"Don't sweat it," Brenda said. "You're the class president. What can they do to you now without looking like jerks and getting into more trouble?"

Jerry wasn't so sure. He hadn't told on them, but the story had leaked out to the assistant principal about how Gabe Marshall and Craig Fox had played horrible, humiliating tricks on Jerry during the campaign for sixth-grade president. That series of tricks had culminated in the chopping off of Jerry's hair. Jerry wondered if they would be mad about their suspension. Would they take it out on him? With their loopy, it's-not-my-fault kind of thinking, would they hold him responsible? Would they torment him even more when they returned today?

Jerry drew in a slow, calming breath and looked

around. He didn't see either of the guys in the crowd of students waiting for the bell to ring. He'd probably run into Craig at the locker they shared. And he was sure to see Gabe in language arts first period. At least, he'd see them both soon and get it over with.

He was suddenly aware that Brenda was talking, and he hadn't been listening.

"I'm so excited!" she said. "It's taken my whole life to get them to say yes. I can't believe they actually agreed to let me get one!"

Jerry nodded. He didn't want Brenda to think he wasn't interested in her, but he had no idea what she was talking about.

"Great," he said.

"So maybe you can come with me when I pick one out," Brenda said.

"Sure," Jerry answered. "Just let me know."

He searched his brain. Pick out what? A new computer? But she already had one. Maybe it was a bike. Or a TV for her room. Or maybe, it was a—

"Just think—a puppy of my very own," she said and sighed.

Jerry grinned. "That's great, Bren." *Relief.* He didn't have to admit to her that he hadn't been listening.

"I guess I finally convinced Mom that I'll take care of it. She'll only have to let it out at noon. I'll do all the rest."

The bell rang, and the crowd of students turned toward the school to begin the regular morning funnel through the school doorway. Jerry felt the press of people on all sides of him.

"*Whoa!*" It was almost a whisper, but Jerry recognized the voice beside him.

He turned to see Cinnamon O'Brien staring through the crowd. She swallowed hard.

"Whoa what?" Jerry asked.

"Who is *that?*" she murmured. "Look at that hair. The humidity doesn't even make it go limp or frizzy. He's *amazing.*"

Jerry and Brenda followed her gaze. A boy—tall, blond, and handsome—stood near the glass door, talking with two other guys as they waited their turn to move into the school. The boy turned and saw his reflection in the door; he tilted his head to one side, smiled a little, and ran a hand through his hair before turning back to his friends.

"You mean the guy in the blue sweater?" Brenda asked. "I don't know who he is, but something tells me he's pretty stuck on himself."

Cinnamon inched forward with the crowd, her eyes wide and blue, and her mouth slightly open. Her voice was full of wonder. "But where has he been since school started? I would've remembered that face, those eyes, that—"

"We get the idea, Cinnamon," Brenda said. "I've never noticed him before this. Maybe he's new."

"Or maybe he's a seventh grader," Jerry offered.

Cinnamon's face lit up. "A *seventh* grader." Her voice dropped even lower. "An older man." Her head swiveled to face Jerry and Brenda. "Do you think a seventh-grade boy would ever be interested in a sixth-grade girl?"

Jerry looked over again at the boy. He apparently said something funny, because his friend laughed, reached out, and gently slapped the top of his head. The handsome boy, who was almost through the door, leaned back to check his reflection once again, frowning. He turned back and said something that Jerry couldn't hear over the clamor. But Jerry could've sworn the kid's lips said, "Watch the hair."

"Don't ask me why," Jerry said, "but I think you two might make an interesting couple."

Cinnamon squealed and bounced next to him. "Really? It would be so cool: me with a *seventh grader*. He would be, like—what do you call those things that make *you* look good and everybody else green with envy? Oh, yeah! A *status symbol*." Her face grew serious. "My goal for today is to find out his name."

They were almost at the school door. The press of the crowd was tighter now.

"Shouldn't be too hard," Jerry said, shrugging. "Why don't you just ask him?"

"Are you kidding?" Cinnamon said, alarmed.

"Then he'd know I was *interested* in him."

Brenda frowned. "But you *are* interested in him. How else would you get to know him?"

Cinnamon looked at Brenda with disbelief. "Not by asking him his name! You find out about a guy by asking his *friends* about him," she said. "By telling them not to tell him, and of course they tell, and *then* he knows you're interested."

Brenda didn't laugh, but Jerry could tell she was using a lot of self-restraint. "Oh, I see," she said, nodding, trying to look serious. "That's how it's done."

"*And,*" Cinnamon said with emphasis, as if she were about to divulge an important tip, "by doing some serious flirting." Brenda didn't respond, so Cinnamon leveled a gaze at her. "You *do* know about flirting, don't you?"

Brenda shrugged. "I've seen *you* do it plenty of times."

Now they were through the door, and students moved off in various directions.

"You mean," Cinnamon said, turning to Brenda, "you're in sixth grade, and you've never personally flirted with a boy? I've known how to flirt practically *forever.*"

Brenda's gaze sharpened. "It's not like I'm socially dysfunctional, Cinnamon. I'd just rather—"

But Cinnamon wasn't listening. She darted away down the hall, probably to follow the blond boy, Jerry figured.

Brenda rolled her eyes. "What an airhead."

Jerry put an arm around her shoulder as they walked. "That's our Cinnamon," he said.

Craig Fox was already at their locker when Jerry arrived.

Jerry could suddenly hear his heart beating. "Hey, Craig," he said, trying to make his voice as light as possible. He watched Craig's face for a hint about what he was thinking.

Craig had not only been half of the team responsible for Jerry's short hair, he had performed the actual hair-cutting while Gabe Marshall held Jerry down on the bathroom floor.

Craig glanced at Jerry's hair, and a small smile curled the edges of his lips. "Me an' Marshall had a great week," he said, throwing his jacket on the bottom of the locker. Jerry decided it might not be the best time to point out that the locker had two hooks for outdoor wear. "We hung out at his house. Played video games and watched game shows on TV."

Jerry thought that sounded spectacularly boring. He also didn't believe a word of it. But he said, "Sounds great."

"Yeah. Wish we could get suspended *every* week." He looked away, over Jerry's shoulder. "Hey, Marshall! Get over here!"

Jerry turned to see Gabe Marshall, Craig's accomplice, loping down the hall toward them. He felt his body stiffen and his pulse race even faster.

"Marshall, look at Flack's hair." Craig laughed loudly. "What a geek!"

Gabe grinned and bobbed his head. "Yeah, Flack, I'd say we did you a big favor by chopping off your hair. The buzz cut you got to fix it is real becoming."

"Thanks," Jerry said. He shrugged and turned back to his locker, hoping he looked unfazed by their taunts. "Oh, Gabe," he said, turning back. "Our committee meeting is today."

Jerry wished he'd never invited Gabe to join the committee he'd formed to come up with good ideas for the sixth grade. But, in a weak moment after the flush of winning the presidency, he'd asked him to join.

"Hunh?" Gabe said.

"The committee meeting," Jerry said. "Remember, I invited you to help us think of cool things for our class."

Gabe's face looked sour. "Forget it, Flack," he said. "I never said I'd join."

Jerry suddenly felt lighter. "Okay." The word popped out, sounding relieved and happy before he had a chance to concentrate on his delivery.

A sudden movement and a cry came from the middle of the hallway. Jerry turned to see a girl trip and stagger into two other people and crash to the floor. Her books and notebooks went flying as students scrambled to get out of the way.

She turned over on the floor, her headband down around her neck and her blond hair tangled in front of her eyes. She sat up and rubbed her elbows. "Ow," she whispered.

Craig Fox seemed to find the scene hysterically funny. "Oh, man, oh man!" he chortled, clapping his hands. "I wish I had that on video!"

Gabe laughed, too, and slapped hands with Craig.

Some students paused to watch; others made a detour around her, but no one stopped to help.

"Here," Jerry said. He stooped and gathered up the girl's books and notebooks.

"Look at that," Gabe said. "One dork helping another. Isn't that sweet?"

"I'd say that's real sweet," Craig said.

"Get lost, you guys," Jerry said.

Get lost, you guys? Where had that come from? The words had tumbled from his mouth without his even thinking about them.

It felt pretty good. Great, in fact.

The boys laughed and headed off down the hall.

"Oh, geez," the girl said in a low voice. She pushed the hair out of her eyes and pulled up the headband. "I *would* have to trip right in front of Gabe Marshall."

"Who cares what they think?" Jerry said, wishing he felt as mature as he sounded. "Gabe and Craig are jerks."

The girl sighed. "Yeah, well, Gabe might be a jerk," she said. "But I'd give anything—" She suddenly looked self-conscious, and the redness in her face deepened. "Never mind."

Jerry was surprised. "You like Gabe? You're kidding, right? He just laughed at you for falling down. You don't mind?"

"Of course I mind," she said. "I want to crawl into a hole somewhere and die." She rolled her eyes. "I know. I always fall for the dreamy guys. I'm so stupid."

"You're Elena Charles, right?"

"Yeah."

Elena got to her feet, and Jerry found himself looking up two inches or more. He hadn't realized before that she was so tall. She accepted the books he held out to her.

"Elena, I'm forming a committee of sixth graders to suggest cool things for our class," he said. "Would you like to join?"

Elena's face opened into a surprised smile. "I'd love to."

"Great. Our first meeting's today, sixth period. I can get you a pass to Mr. Hooten's room."

"I'll be there. Thanks for the help."

"Sure. See you."

She turned and trudged back down the hall. Her toes pointed out just a little when she walked and made her gait look somewhat ducklike.

Jerry watched her go. Elena was in a few of his classes. But he'd never talked with her before today.

He had an odd sense of *déjà vu* as she disappeared into the throng of students. There was something very familiar about her. For some reason, he'd never really paid attention to her before, and he didn't know why. She seemed nice. And smart. And she was even pretty.

What was it about Elena?

Then it hit him. Of course! He hadn't really noticed her before this because, even though she was tall, she had a tendency to fade into the background. And that's why he had a familiar feeling about her.

She reminded Jerry of *himself* one month ago, just before school started. She had a lot going for her. But Gabe and Craig had been right about one thing.

She was kind of a dork.

Chapter Two

Jerry met Brenda outside their language arts classroom.

"I just saw Craig and Gabe," Jerry said. "They said they had a great time during their suspension. Claimed they played video games and watched TV the whole time."

"Yeah, right."

"I didn't believe it, either," Jerry said. "But at least they didn't pull any of their tricks on me. Not yet, anyway."

Brenda waved her hand, as if she could wave away his worry. "They're already in trouble for all the stuff they did to you during the campaign. They wouldn't dare try anything else."

Jerry nodded. "I hope you're right."

They walked into the room and took their seats in the front, Brenda in the first row, Jerry right behind her. More than half the students had already arrived; they were talking and getting out their notebooks and pens.

Zoey Long entered, wearing dark sunglasses, and strode to her desk in the back of the room. As usual, she didn't speak to anyone. But nearly every student turned to watch her, as they always did.

Zoey had transferred to Hawthorne Middle School a few weeks ago from Hollywood, where she'd been friends with some of the most famous movie and rock stars in the business. The kids at Hawthorne thought she was the coolest human being they'd ever seen.

Jerry wondered if Zoey wore the dark glasses so she could hide behind them. It would have to be uncomfortable living every day in the focused glare of everyone's attention.

Zoey collapsed into her seat, slid her legs out in front of her, and folded her arms across her chest.

"I wonder about Zoey," Brenda whispered. "Do you think she's lonely?"

Jerry frowned. It was impossible to tell if Zoey was looking at him.

"That's a good question," he said in a low voice, turning back to Brenda. "She's always alone."

Just then, Cinnamon breezed in, flounced back

to her seat next to Zoey, and began whispering in Zoey's ear. Zoey didn't move or even acknowledge that she was listening. For all Jerry knew, she'd fallen asleep behind those dark glasses.

"She's alone, that is, unless Cinnamon's chattering at her," Brenda said. "They make a weird pair. Cinnamon's the only person who has the nerve to approach her."

Gabe Marshall loped into the room and stopped front and center. "I'm back," he announced, spreading his hands in front of him. "You may all applaud."

A few students laughed and clapped. Jerry was surprised it was so few.

"Nobody cares, Gabe," Cinnamon called out. "Give it a rest."

Jerry noticed that Cinnamon sneaked a peek sideways to see if Zoey approved of her sarcastic remark. She was rewarded with Zoey's smirk.

So she was awake, after all.

Gabe looked as if he was about to say something sarcastic in return but changed his mind. He closed his mouth and dropped into his seat. He looked over at Jerry.

"Hey, thanks for the vacation, Flack," he said. "Fox and I partied every day. It was so cool."

Jerry forced a smile. "Don't mention it, Gabe." He was happy that he'd said it with a casual air, as if he didn't care one way or the other.

Ms. Robertson, their language arts teacher, arrived just as the bell rang.

"Good morning," she said. She took attendance and began class. "We're going to start a new unit today. We'll be talking about William Shakespeare and reading one of his plays—A *Midsummer Night's Dream*."

Jerry had never read anything by Shakespeare, but he'd heard of the play.

Cinnamon spoke up from the back of the room. "Oh, yeah, Shakespeare. Didn't he live like a thousand years ago or something?"

"Not that long ago," Ms. Robertson answered. "This play was written around 1595."

"Why can't we read something, like, that happens now?" Robin Hedges asked in a whiny voice.

"We've read some modern short stories," Ms. Robertson said, "but Shakespeare's one of the greatest writers the world has ever known. You should be familiar with some of his work."

A few grumbles were heard around the room.

"Shakespeare was also a poet and an actor," Ms. Robertson said, ignoring them. "But he was best known for writing plays. A *Midsummer Night's Dream* has a little bit of everything. It has four protagonists who fall in love, quarrel, and make up; a forest full of sprites and fairies who play tricks on humans; and a motley band of actors who rehearses a silly play and performs it for the nobility."

Ms. Robertson continued. "This is an interesting period—" She looked up and stopped. "Yes, Robin?"

"Do we have to take notes on this?" Robin asked.

"On what?"

"On what you're saying."

Ms. Robertson frowned. "No, Robin, but I'm telling you that this is an interesting period in history. Shakespeare was writing during the reign of Queen Elizabeth the First, and this time became known as the Elizabethan Era. We're going to be learning about what life was like during Elizabethan times. And, in fact, starting tomorrow, we're going to have after-school classes for anyone who's interested."

Robin groaned. "Do we have to go?"

"No, you don't have to go," Ms. Robertson said. "But—"

"Will our grade go down if we don't go?" Robin asked.

"No, your grade won't go down," Ms. Robertson said with an impatient edge to her voice. "But don't you want to hear what the classes are?"

"What?" Jerry blurted it out. He wanted to hear.

"An instructor—a friend of mine—will be here to teach you about stage combat—"

"Cool!" Gabe shouted. "We're really gonna fight? And not get in trouble?"

"Well," Ms. R. said, "I think you'll learn that you're not really fighting when you participate in stage combat. It's a discipline that you practice with partners.

"We'll also learn about the food Elizabethans ate and the clothes they wore."

"Hmm," Cinnamon said. Jerry thought it sounded like an interested *hmm*. Cinnamon was attracted to anything having to do with fashion.

"During the sixteenth century people amused themselves at festivals, where there were jugglers, puppeteers, minstrels, madrigal singers, and lots of food. We'll be having sessions in these things, as well."

Jerry turned back to see that now even Robin looked vaguely interested.

Ms. Robertson passed out copies of *A Midsummer Night's Dream*. "Tonight, I'd like you to read act one, scene one," she said. "We'll start out slowly. You'll see notes written at the bottom of the pages to help you understand the language.

"In this scene, we meet the four protagonists: Hermia and Lysander, who are in love; and Helena, who's in love with Demetrius. But Demetrius doesn't love her; he's in love with Hermia, Lysander's lover."

"Weird names," Cinnamon murmured.

Ms. Robertson smiled. "You'll get them all straight when you start reading. We'll talk about this first scene tomorrow."

* * *

"I told you I'd do it!" Cinnamon cried. "I found out his name!" She rushed up to Jerry and Brenda who stood at the back of the cafeteria line.

"Whose name?" Jerry asked.

"*'Whose name?'* Only that fabulously gorgeous guy we saw right before school started!" she said. "How can you forget? Remember? That cute blond guy?"

Brenda nudged him, grinning. "Yeah, Jerry, how can you forget that cute blond guy?"

"Oh, yeah," Jerry said. He picked up a tray and utensils. "So what's his name?"

Cinnamon said it slowly, as if to savor every sound. "It's Sandy Powers." She beamed and bounced. "And you were right; he's a *seventh grader*. I asked one of his friends and told him not to tell I asked. But by the way he sort of smiled, I could tell he'd go straight to Sandy to tell him."

"Good strategy . . . I guess," Brenda said. She took a small bowl of macaroni and cheese from the woman wearing a hairnet behind the food counter, then picked up a dish of soggy green beans. "So did you flirt with him yet?"

"No, but that's the next thing in my Get-Sandy-Powers-to-notice-me project."

"Well, good luck," Jerry said, paying for his lunch.

"I'm a project person," Cinnamon said. "I just realized that. Have you noticed? I always have some cool thing I'm working on, and it usually involves a guy." She paid for her lunch.

Jerry turned with his tray toward his usual table.

Halfway across the cafeteria, he saw Elena Charles enter. She turned and glanced over her shoulder, as if she'd heard her name called, and plowed right into Gabe Marshall. Jerry took in a breath. She put a hand to her mouth and gestured apologetically to Gabe, who made an angry face. He said a few words, and her face crumpled as if she was about to cry. She turned and hurried away, her face blazing red.

Poor Elena. One embarrassment a day is more than enough for anyone, but she'd looked clutzy twice in just a few hours. And in front of the boy she had a crush on. Jerry knew exactly how she felt, and his chest ached in sympathy for her.

Jerry and Brenda went to their table, where Kim and Kat Henley were already sitting with Tony Bridges and Chad Newsome.

Over the heads in the cafeteria, Jerry saw Cinnamon hurry over and sit with Zoey. Students at nearby tables sneaked glances at Zoey and copied her slouch. Jerry figured they thought if they *looked* as cool as Zoey, they might *become* as cool as she was. This copycat behavior had started as soon as Zoey had moved here three weeks ago and was still going on. It was a very interesting social phenomenon, Jerry thought. He sat down next to Brenda.

"Hey, guys," Kim said from across the table. "Is your language arts class going to read *A Midsummer Night's Dream*?"

"And take those classes after school on Elizabethan stuff?" Kat asked.

"Yeah," Jerry said. "All the sixth graders are doing the same thing."

"I want to learn how to juggle," Kim said, "or learn about the clothes."

Kat smiled. "I'd rather sing in a madrigal group."

Kim turned to her sister. "But you can't carry a tune. You'd just mess everybody up."

"I can *so* carry a tune!" Kat said. "Didn't you hear me singing in the shower this morning?"

"Yes, I did. I rest my case." Kim took a bite of her sugar cookie.

"What are you *talking* about?" Kat demanded. "I sounded really good! Professional even."

"I don't want to crush your dreams of singing stardom, so I'll say no more." Kim pretended to zip her lips together.

"*What!*"

Jerry saw Tony and Chad grin at each other across the table. If the sisters' constant arguing didn't drive you crazy, they could be somewhat entertaining.

Jerry sat up tall and watched Zoey again through the crowd. He said, "Brenda and I were kind of watching Zoey this morning. Don't you think it's weird that she's idolized by everybody, but she doesn't seem to have any friends?"

"Hey, yeah," Kat said. "You're right. People watch her from a distance and hope she notices them, but they don't talk to her."

"Well, she gives the impression that she's not very friendly," Tony spoke up.

Brenda added, "She doesn't smile much."

Jerry picked up his fork and scooped up some macaroni and cheese from his plate. "It's amazing that someone can be so popular and not have any friends."

"Of course, there's Cinnamon," Kim said. "But then she kind of foists herself on Zoey."

"Do you guys know Elena Charles?" Jerry said, looking around the table at his friends. "She seems really nice."

"I know who she is, but I've never talked to her, other than saying hi," Brenda said. "She's in our science class."

"And our computer class," Tony added. "She's pretty quiet."

"She seems kind of shy," Chad said.

Brenda leaned in. "Maybe she needs more self-confidence."

Jerry nodded. "I talked to her this morning and invited her to join the sixth-grade committee."

"Hey, good idea," Brenda said.

Jerry sat up. An idea was forming in his mind.

Brenda gave him a questioning look, but he just smiled and took another bite of macaroni.

Yeah, he thought. This could be very interesting.

Chapter Three

*J*erry looked around at the students on his Make Sixth Grade the Coolest committee and felt happy. It was made up of his favorite people: Brenda, Kim and Kat, Tony, Chad, and Elena. He didn't know Elena well, but the others were people who cared about the school and usually had good ideas. He figured Elena would be a great member of the committee, too. He'd also included Emily Lloyd, who'd been elected sixth-grade vice president; and Lauren Michelson, the sixth-grade secretary. Jerry's science teacher, Mr. Hooten, would act as sponsor of the group.

"Jerry, I think you should be commended for actually setting up this committee and honoring a campaign promise," Kat said.

"Yeah, real politicians don't do that much," Kim added. "They just lie during the campaign to look good and then do whatever they want after they're elected."

"Well, the reason I ran for president was to do some cool things for the class," Jerry said, shrugging. "And more people have more ideas."

"Makes sense," Kat said.

"So." Jerry smiled. "Let's hear your ideas. Lauren, will you take notes?"

"Notes?" She blinked.

"Write down the ideas."

Kim leaned over to her. "You're the secretary," she said in a low voice. "Remember?"

"Oh, sure." Lauren's cheeks colored. "Duh. I guess I forgot that a secretary takes *notes*."

"No problem," Jerry said. "Okay. What should we work on this year? Anyone have ideas to discuss?"

"I really like your idea of e-mail stations in the cafeteria," Brenda said. She turned to Mr. Hooten. "Do you think we could do that?"

"I don't know," Mr. Hooten said. "I'm sure the media center wouldn't want us to take any of their computers."

"So I guess we'd have to get a couple of new ones," Jerry responded.

Mr. Hooten nodded. "You'd have to raise money for that."

"We could do it." Jerry looked around the table. "Does anyone have an idea for a money-making project?"

"A bake sale?" Lauren suggested. "Or am I supposed to be quiet and just take notes?"

"No, no," Jerry said. "That's a good suggestion. Thanks. Anyone else?"

"We need a big project that people will come to," Brenda said.

"Yeah, and pay money to get in the door," said Kim.

"Like a play," Elena said, "or a dance."

"Something fun," Tony added.

"If we want to make money, we should do something that brings in more than just the sixth graders," Brenda added, "but something our class could organize."

Tony cleared his throat. "Well, the sixth graders are going to all those classes after school to learn about Elizabethan stuff. Could we do a bake sale with that as a theme?"

"I've got it!" Brenda said, her face brightening. "You gave me the idea, Tony. What about an Elizabethan festival? Remember, Ms. R. said that people went to fairs all the time back then. They watched jugglers and puppeteers and minstrels and stuff. What if we put on a festival and invited the seventh and eighth graders?"

"And families and friends," Jerry said. "Yeah, we

could do that." He looked at Mr. Hooten. "You think Ms. Robertson would like that idea?"

"She just might," he said, nodding slowly. "I'll check with her before I leave this afternoon."

Jerry smiled. He'd been president for less than two weeks, and already they were doing something cool for his class.

Jerry decided he just might have to rethink his earlier decision never to go into politics.

"Okay, Bren," Jerry said on the way to computer class later that afternoon. "I have this idea, and I want to see what you think."

"Sure," Brenda said. "What is it?"

Jerry looked around at the students in the hallway and lowered his voice.

"Well, first I was thinking about how much power Zoey seems to have with everyone."

"Yeah. Kids are still slouching and slumping all over the place, imitating her."

"And you know how no one seems to notice what a great person Elena is? I didn't want to say this at lunch, but people probably think she's kind of a dork."

"I'd go that far," Brenda agreed.

"So what if Zoey gave Elena some attention? I mean, in front of everybody? Don't you think people would think if Zoey talks to her, she must be a cool person?"

A smile spread across Brenda's face. "What a good idea! Wouldn't it be great if Zoey's attention could get people interested in Elena?"

"Yeah," Jerry said. "Maybe I'll ask Zoey if she'd like to try an experiment."

"She has to know how much her opinion counts around here."

"I'm not going to make a big deal of it," Jerry said. "I'll just casually mention that it might be fun to see if she can elevate Elena's status around school, and all she'd have to do is talk to her."

"If Zoey's as bored as she acts," Brenda said, "she'll do it just to relieve the monotony."

"I hope so. And who knows? Maybe Zoey will actually make a friend. I'll talk to her after school. Her locker's just across the hall from mine."

"That was a great idea, Brenda," Elena said after computer class. Brenda and Elena stood with Jerry in the hallway as students charged out of classrooms, heading for their lockers. "I mean, the Elizabethan festival. I bet we could get a lot of people to come. My aunt's a reporter for the newspaper; maybe she'd even come and write an article about it."

"That'd be cool," Jerry said. "But let's wait and see what Ms. R. thinks of the festival first."

Elena's cheeks turned pink, and she laughed. "Oh, right. I'm always racing ahead on everything."

A hand reached out from the crowd, and knuckles scrubbed hard on the top of Jerry's head.

"Ow," Jerry said, reaching up to stop whoever was hurting him.

"Hey, Flack!"

Jerry turned to see Gabe walking away from him. Gabe turned around, walking backward, and hollered, "Yeah, I'd say we did you a favor, Flack! That hair is so great! Like a brush with really short bristles all over your head. It's so—*you.*"

Jerry opened his mouth to call out something clever. But nothing clever came to mind, so he closed it.

Several students nearby laughed as Gabe vanished into the crowd.

"Will this ever *end?*" Brenda said. "I'm so sick of Gabe harassing Jerry, I could scream!"

Jerry felt his face heating up. He wished he'd thought of something funny to say back to Gabe.

"It happened so fast," he mumbled.

Jerry saw Elena gazing into the distance where Gabe had disappeared. She sighed deeply.

There was no doubt about it. Elena was interested in Gabe.

Very interested.

How could she have a crush on someone like Gabe? She was so nice, and he was such a jerk.

Jerry was totally mystified.

* * *

"Hey, Zoey."

Zoey stood at her locker, shoving books onto the top shelf. The hall was noisy and crowded with students opening and slamming lockers.

Zoey nodded at Jerry. She pulled a denim jacket out of her locker and closed it.

"I have an idea that might be kind of interesting," Jerry said.

Zoey's face didn't change. "What?"

Several students turned with curious glances. It was always news when Zoey actually talked to other people.

"Let's walk outside," Jerry said, lowering his voice.

They walked to the door, pushed it open, and strolled out into the crisp autumn air. Jerry led her to the oak where he always met Brenda before school.

"Do you know Elena Charles?"

"Who?"

"Elena Charles."

"No."

"She's a sixth grader," Jerry said.

Zoey leaned against the tree. "Okay. So . . . ?"

"I'm not surprised that you don't know her," Jerry said, "because she kind of fades into the background. But she's very nice, and she's smart and kind of—"

"Bottom line," Zoey said, gazing away.

"What?"

Zoey looked back at Jerry and stared at him. "Where's this going?"

Jerry felt uncomfortable under her stare.

He hurried on. "I just thought that . . . well, I mean . . . it would be really great . . . really *interesting* if you could give Elena some attention, so—"

"Attention?"

"Yeah. Because I think you could help people notice her. You see, because she's kind of, well, sort of what you might call a dork."

"What everyone calls you."

"Well, yeah."

"Only they're wrong."

Jerry blinked. Had he heard her right? Zoey had told him after his campaign speech for sixth-grade president not long ago that he was "unbelievably cool." But at this precise moment, he was standing in front of her—just after Gabe had scrubbed his knuckles into his head—and he was stammering and feeling very uncool. So her comment surprised him.

"Well, thank you, Zoey."

"Sometimes you have dorklike tendencies, but . . ." Her voice trailed off for a moment. "You can be something of a rebel when the situation calls for it."

"Me?" Jerry was astounded. "A *rebel*?"

Zoey looked him in the eye. "You're stronger

than you think you are, Flack."

Jerry blinked again.

"Look how you were treated during the election," she said, "but you stood your ground."

"Oh. I hadn't thought of that."

"That took guts."

"Well, thank you," Jerry said. "I guess sometimes it takes someone else to point out our strengths."

Zoey shrugged. "Three years in therapy."

"Therapy?"

"In California. Taught me a lot."

"Oh." Jerry didn't know what to say to that. "Well, anyway, about Elena—"

"I'll do it."

"I just think . . ." Jerry stopped. "You'll do it? You'll talk to Elena in public?"

"Yeah."

"That's fantastic!" Jerry beamed. He hadn't even had to talk her into it.

"Point her out sometime," Zoey said. She pushed off from the tree and headed across the school grounds.

"Hey, thanks, Zoey!" Jerry called after her.

She didn't turn around or respond.

She certainly is an interesting person, Jerry thought, watching her go. Definitely a woman of few words.

And full of surprises.

* * *

Jerry walked back into the school and met Brenda on her way out.

"Want to walk a few blocks till you turn off?" he asked.

"Sure. Did you talk to Zoey?"

They left the building and passed the oak. "She's going to do it," Jerry said.

"Great!"

"It was easy. No discussion."

Brenda nodded. "I don't think Zoey discusses." Something caught her eye, and she nudged Jerry. "Looks like Cinnamon's making fast work of her plan to get that seventh grader to notice her." She nodded past a pine tree, toward the corner of the building.

Jerry turned and looked.

Cinnamon stood next to Sandy Powers, who leaned his shoulder against the brick building in a cool pose, a hand slid into his back pocket.

Brenda frowned thoughtfully. "Look at her weird body language."

Cinnamon pivoted first one way and then the other, laughing and twisting a strand of hair around her finger.

"She's flirting," Jerry said.

"Yeah," Brenda agreed. "She looks as if she's trying to dance without moving her feet."

Jerry smiled. "Happens in all species, I guess. The dance, I mean."

Brenda thought a moment. "But she looks dumb. Why do guys like it when girls twist and move around like that?"

Jerry shrugged. "Some guys like flirts, I guess."

Brenda looked back at Jerry and frowned. "Would you like it if I did that?"

Cinnamon shrieked then, laughed, and covered her mouth with both hands. She gave Sandy a playful shove, and he grinned and moved closer.

"It would be out of character for you to act like that, Bren," Jerry said. "I'd wonder what was wrong with you."

"Yeah, no kidding," Brenda said.

They walked along in silence for a while. Jerry was always surprised that they could let whole minutes pass between them, and it was never uncomfortable; he never felt as if he had to fill the silences with talk, the way he did with some people. That was a mark of a very good friend, he thought. A very good girlfriend.

They crossed the street at the edge of the school grounds and headed down the sidewalk.

Brenda suddenly stopped. "Hey, look."

"What?" Jerry looked where Brenda pointed.

A small black-and-white puppy romped across the street ahead of them, its tongue hanging out the side of its mouth. It turned to see Jerry and Brenda and ran joyfully to them, ears and tail flying.

"Well, hello," Brenda said, laughing and leaning down to pet the pooch. "Who do you belong to, sweetie?" She looked up at Jerry, frowning. "Jerry, this puppy's skin and bones."

"Poor dog." Jerry reached down to pat its head. "And no tag. Not even a collar."

Brenda kneeled on the sidewalk, and the pup leaped up to lick her face, wriggling all over, turning itself into a comma one way and then the other. "Boy, are you cute. You're an all-American pup, aren't you? No specific breed, but a special mixture of adorable and sweet."

The puppy rolled over on its back, and Brenda obliged with tummy scratches.

Brenda looked around. "I don't see anybody who could be the owner. You think she's a stray?"

"I don't know. Maybe she got away from her owner."

"Let's ask around," Brenda suggested.

"Okay."

Brenda gathered the pup in her arms, and they walked up the front sidewalk of the house closest to them. Jerry knocked on the door, while the puppy squirmed in Brenda's arms. After a moment, the door was pulled open by an elderly woman.

"Hello."

"Sorry to bother you," Brenda said, "but is this your puppy?"

The woman smiled. "No, I've never seen it before. Pretty cute, but it could use a good meal to fatten it up a bit."

"That's what we thought," Brenda said. "Are there any families with kids around here?"

"Just across the street," she said, nodding at a brown ranch-style house. "But I happen to know that the mother's allergic to dogs. They'd never get one."

"Thanks," Brenda said. They turned away, and she was grinning. "You see what this means, Jerry? We can't very well abandon this poor little puppy. I'm going to take her home. Mom and Dad have already agreed that I could get a pup. They'll love her!"

"They'd have to have hearts made of stone not to," Jerry said. "Who could resist her?"

"You hear that, puppy? You're going to be *mine!*" She looked at Jerry. "She's so skinny, she obviously doesn't belong to anybody."

"*Hey, you found my dog!*"

Jerry looked up to see Craig Fox ambling down the sidewalk toward them.

"Oh, no," Brenda murmured.

"This is your dog?" Jerry asked.

"Yeah, it got away from me yesterday," Craig said. "I've been lookin' all over for it."

Brenda held the puppy closer. "Craig, this poor thing is starving! And why didn't you get a tag and collar?"

Craig shrugged. "I've only had it for two days. Give me a break. It ran away before I had a chance."

Brenda's eyes narrowed. "You don't seem the puppy type."

Craig laughed. "Whatdaya mean? I like dogs! Here, give it to me."

Brenda hugged the puppy even closer. "Tell me what you named it."

"Pooch."

"*Pooch!*" She gave Craig an angry look. "Male or female?"

Craig scowled. "What's it to ya? Give it to me." He reached for the puppy.

"I don't think this is your dog," Brenda said, turning away and putting herself between the puppy and Craig. "You don't even know whether it's a male or female."

"What are you talkin' about?"

"*Male or female?*"

One second passed. "Female," Craig said. Brenda's face fell, and he grinned. "I *told* you, she's mine. Give her to me. Come here, Pooch."

Brenda gave Jerry a pleading look. Jerry's heart ached for Brenda and the puppy. "We'll walk home with you," Jerry said finally, "and you can show us the receipt."

Craig snorted. "What receipt? I got her from a friend of my dad's. Look, she's *mine*, okay? Hand her over." He took the puppy from Brenda.

Brenda's eyes filled with tears. "I don't believe this poor puppy is yours," she said, "but you'd better take good care of her, Craig. She's so sweet and trusting. You'd better feed her and walk her—"

"Yeah, yeah," Craig said. He held up the puppy's front paw. "Say bye-bye, Poochie."

He turned and hurried down the sidewalk, laughing.

Brenda whirled around to Jerry. "She doesn't belong to Craig, Jerry! He was calling her *it* until he guessed she was a female."

Jerry felt heartsick. "I'm sorry, Bren," he said, shaking his head. He looked at Craig's back as he walked down the street. "I bet you're right."

"What are we going to do?" Brenda asked.

"I don't know," Jerry answered. "But don't worry; we'll do something."

Chapter Four

*J*erry had thought about the pup ever since he'd left Brenda that afternoon. Brenda was right. It was obvious, especially looking back on it, that the little dog didn't belong to Craig.

Jerry kept asking himself why he let Craig take the pup. It had happened so fast. Jerry wasn't a confrontational person. And Craig had guessed that the pup was a female. But that's what it was: a guess. Jerry was sure of it.

After Craig had taken the pup away, Jerry had wrapped his arm around Brenda and walked her home.

"What kind of a pet owner would Craig be?" she'd cried to Jerry. "He has no compassion, no kindness that I can see. He loves it when people are embarrassed or doing crazy things. He lives in chaos, at least at school. How's he going to take care of that sweet, defenseless animal?"

"Maybe his mom will take care of her," Jerry said.

"But how do we *know* that?"

Jerry sighed. "We don't."

Jerry felt awful for Brenda, but he felt worse for the little dog. Brenda was right: Craig wasn't responsible enough to take care of a living creature.

Jerry ate dinner that night with his family, but his mind kept drifting away from the conversation.

"Why can't you help us?" six-year-old Melissa whined at her mother. "We need you! This project is *important*."

"Honey, I told you," their mother said patiently. She pulled out another piece of pizza from the open box on the middle of the table. "I have a heavy load of classes to teach this semester. I'd love to help out with your play, but I just can't manage another thing at the moment. You shouldn't have told your teacher you'd do a play for Performance Day without asking me first."

Melissa scowled. "But none of the other mothers can do it, either. I guess we'll just have to do it ourselves."

Jerry was only vaguely following the conversation. He'd decided to call Craig tonight and talk to him. Maybe he could persuade him to give up the dog. Brenda was right: Craig wasn't a puppy person. He probably didn't really want her, anyway.

"I'm sorry, honey," his mother repeated from across the table. "Why don't you think of another project? Something simpler. I could help if it would take less time."

"Sorry, Melissa," their dad cut in. "I'm also busy. But I could help with a smaller project, too. Something we could work on after dinner."

Melissa's lower lip grew long as she looked at her plate. "But I want to be in a play." She sniffled and wiped her nose with her index finger.

Mrs. Flack stared over the table thoughtfully. "Melissa, what if I find someone else to help you with your play?"

Melissa gazed up at her mother with new hope in her eyes. "Who?"

Mrs. Flack's gaze turned to Jerry, who was thinking about how he would approach Craig. "Craig?" he'd say. "Do you really want to take care of the pup for the next fifteen years or so?"

Fifteen years sounded like forever. Maybe Craig would decide he really didn't want the pup after all.

"Jerry? Did you hear me?" his mother asked.

He looked over at her. "What?"

"Off in outer space," his dad said around a mouthful of pizza.

"Melissa, I have a better idea than a play," his mom said. "Jerry could show you some science tricks that you and your friends could perform."

Melissa screwed up her face. "No. I want a play. Science tricks aren't exciting."

Jerry glanced at his sister. "Every science trick I know is exciting."

"That's what you think," Melissa muttered.

Jerry's mom sighed. "Jerry, would you consider spending some time working with Melissa and her friends on a play?"

Jerry looked around the table and blinked. "Me? Why? What do you mean, a play? Like a theater play?"

"Melissa's teacher wants the kids to think of a project they can do for Performance Day in about two weeks," his mother said. "Some children are going to draw pictures and show them. Some will sing songs or tell stories or recite poems."

"And me and my friends want to put on a play," Melissa said.

Jerry frowned. "Melissa, I don't know anything about directing plays. And I know a lot about science."

"I don't want science," Melissa said.

"Why not?"

"We always do science around here," she said. "I want to try something *new*."

"Directing a play shouldn't be hard," his dad said. "You just direct traffic while they say their lines."

Jerry knew there must be more to it than that.

But he gazed over at his sister, who was watching him, her eyes imploring him to say yes.

"Please, Jerry? You're not as good as a mom, but we could stand you for a little while."

"Trying to get on my good side, Missy?"

"Please?"

Jerry sighed heavily. "Okay. I guess I could do it. But what play would we do?"

"We'll make it up," Melissa said, brightening. "Me and my friends will do it."

"I'll supervise, but you guys will have to come up with the play."

"*Yay!*"

Jerry looked at his mother. "I need to make a phone call now. Mind if I leave the table?"

"Go ahead," his mother said. "You've earned the right to do whatever you like tonight." She smiled. "Thank you for agreeing to help."

"Sure."

Jerry got up and took the stairs two at a time to the second floor. He went into his parents' room and pulled the phone directory out of his mother's bedside table.

Flopping on the floor, he opened the directory. His hand shook a little as his finger traced down the list of Foxes in town. A lot was riding on this phone call. He took a deep breath and dialed.

The phone was answered. "Yeah?" said a low voice.

"Uh, Mr. Fox?" Jerry asked.

"Yeah, who is it?" The voice was gruff.

"This is Jerry Flack. I'm in your son's class?" He waited to see if Craig's dad would make a noise indicating that he was listening. He didn't.

"Um, I just wanted to talk to Craig about his new dog," Jerry said.

"We don't have a dog."

"You don't?"

"Why would I want a mangy mutt that eats our food and pees all over the place?"

"Oh." Jerry faltered a moment. Could Craig have the pup in the house without his dad even knowing? "Um, well, I just wanted to talk to him. To Craig, I mean. Not the dog."

"He isn't here," Craig's dad said.

"Okay, well, thank you. Bye." Jerry was happy to end the conversation. He hung up the phone and sat back against the bed. How could Craig have a dog—a pup that barks and whines and runs around the house—without his dad knowing it?

Craig must be keeping her somewhere else, Jerry thought. But where? It'd be hard to find a good place where she wouldn't be discovered.

Jerry thought about the poor little dog, hidden away in some cold, dark place.

He didn't know where she was. But he knew for sure that Craig wasn't giving her everything she needed: scratches and petting and playing and walks in the fresh air and food and water and love.

A big hollow space opened inside Jerry's chest. He was responsible for the pup. He should never have allowed Craig to take her away from Brenda.

But he'd make it right, he thought. He'd figure out a way to get the pup away from Craig. Then he'd give her to Brenda.

Just as soon as he found out where Craig had her hidden.

"Hey, Melissa," Jerry called out. He'd stuck his head out his bedroom door. The light was on in his sister's room. "Come here. I want to show you something."

"I'm busy."

"Want to see a science trick?"

"Nope."

Jerry sighed. "It'll only take a second."

"One," Melissa said. "There. That's a second."

"But you didn't come in here. Just give me one minute." No answer. "You want me to help you with your play, right?"

He heard Melissa huff. "O-*kay*. But it had better be good."

She appeared in her bedroom doorway, then trudged down the hall and into Jerry's room.

"Okay," Jerry said, smiling. He followed her. "This is a good one. See this dollar bill?" He held up a brand-new bill.

Melissa rolled her eyes. "Well, duh."

"Okay, I'm going to drop it. All you have to do is catch it. Like this."

Jerry's fingers let the bill go, and with his other hand, an inch underneath, he grabbed it.

"Now I'll drop the money, and if you can catch it in your fingers without moving your hand, you can have it."

Jerry was surprised when the pupils of Melissa's eyes grew larger. Wow. Melissa was greedier than he thought.

"You really mean that?" she asked.

"Yup," he said. "Okay, put your hand just an inch below mine."

When her hand was in the right place, he dropped the dollar bill. It sailed past her fingers before she closed them to catch it.

"Oh!" she cried. "Let me try again."

"One more time."

He dropped the dollar bill a second time, and once again, it sliced the air between her fingers before she caught it.

Melissa scowled. "Not fair. It's a trick of some kind."

Jerry smiled. "It's not exactly a trick. It's just that it takes longer for you to see it drop, for your brain to react, and send the message to your fingers to close. By the time you're ready to catch it, it's passed your fingers."

"That's rotten."

"But, see? You could show some great science tricks to your class, instead of putting on a play. Wouldn't that be fun?"

"No. I want to do the play."

Jerry thought of something. "Want to keep the dollar?"

"Nice try, Jerry," Melissa said, "but bribing me won't work. We're putting on a play, and you said you'd help."

Jerry sighed. "Okay." He folded the dollar and shoved it into his pocket. "We'll do the play."

Jerry spotted Brenda waiting for him at the tree in front of the school. As usual, crowds of students milled around, waiting for the bell to ring.

He'd just opened his mouth to say hello when a loud voice behind him giggled loudly and said, "Sandy Powers, your hair is *amazing*. How do you get it so wavy and full of body?"

Jerry turned to see Cinnamon reach up and touch Sandy's hair. She giggled again.

Sandy smiled and shrugged. "I don't do anything to it," he said. He smoothed his hair with his palm. "It just does that naturally." He touched her hair. "Yours is thick and wavy, too."

"Yeah, I know, but I have to use a curling iron on it every single morning; it's a major pain. You're lucky yours is natural." She smiled and wrapped a strand of her hair around her finger. "Great hair is wasted on a guy."

He grinned. "I wouldn't say *wasted*."

Brenda leaned closer to Jerry. "At least they have stimulating conversations," she murmured.

Jerry laughed.

"Our language arts class is having these sessions after school about how people lived a long time ago?" Cinnamon said. "I mean, back around the time Abraham Lincoln was president?"

Brenda whispered, "Only about two hundred and fifty years off. And in a different country."

"So, I guess I'm going to take the class on Elizabethan clothing," Cinnamon said. "It's pretty cool to find out what people thought was fashionable back then." She smiled. "The picture on the front of the playbook shows some guys in *tights*. I wonder what you'd look like in tights." She laughed loudly again.

"I don't know." Sandy grinned. "I wouldn't like wearing 'em, I know that."

"Yeah, tights look better on girls," Cinnamon said. "That is, if their legs have a nice shape."

"Yeah."

Jerry smiled at Brenda. He didn't really mean to eavesdrop, but it was hard not to; they were standing so close.

"I called Craig's house last night," Jerry said.

Brenda perked up. "You did?"

"I wanted to tell Craig about all the stuff he'll have to do if he has a dog. You know, taking her to the vet, feeding her, bathing her, playing with her. I mean, Craig's kind of a lazy guy, and I thought if he knew what's required to take care of a dog, maybe he wouldn't want to keep her."

"Good idea. What happened?"

"His dad answered the phone and told me they don't *have* a dog. Made it pretty clear he doesn't want one, either."

"Really? That's strange." Brenda frowned. "Where could Craig be keeping her?"

"I don't know," Jerry answered. "I'll see Craig today, and if my plan works, he'll give her to us."

"Oh, Jerry, wouldn't that be wonderful? I didn't sleep very well last night, thinking about her."

A shadow appeared in Jerry's peripheral vision. He turned to see Zoey standing next to him, blocking the sun.

"Hey, Zoey," he said.

She nodded. "Want to point out the girl?"

He checked around him to make sure that no one was eavesdropping. He didn't see anyone, but he lowered his voice. "You mean Elena? Sure."

"There she is," Brenda said. "Standing alone next to the flagpole."

"Navy jacket?" Zoey asked.

"Yeah," Jerry said.

"Okay." Zoey strolled off in that direction.

Jerry watched her. Several students turned to see where Zoey was going. She stopped casually next to Elena and spoke to her. The students watched them and whispered to one another. Zoey was actually approaching and *talking* to someone.

"Well, anyway," Brenda said, "good luck with Craig. Let me know how it goes."

"Hey, Craig." Jerry had found him at their locker. Craig had thrown his jacket on the bottom of the locker again. As usual, he didn't pull out any books or notebooks. He never did. He'd jammed two notebooks into the locker every which way the first day of school, their pages bent and dirty, and he hadn't touched them since.

"Oh, you know that little dog you have?" Jerry asked.

"Yeah."

"Well, there's a park across town that lets you take your dog off the leash. I bet—uh, Pooch—that's her name? I bet she'd really like that."

"Oh. Yeah." Craig didn't look interested.

"So what do you feed her?" Jerry took out the notebooks he'd need for the morning and closed the locker.

Craig shrugged. "Stuff. Why?"

"I don't know. I was just thinking about how much time and money it takes to take care of a dog. Did you take her to the vet?"

Craig frowned. "Why?"

"She should be checked over to make sure she's okay."

"She's okay."

"She'll need shots. And a license. It can get expensive."

Craig scowled. "I'm takin' care of her."

"Are you sure you want a dog, Craig? Because Brenda could take really good care of her."

"Forget it." Craig's face opened into a nasty grin. "She's mine." He turned to go.

"Where are you keeping her, Craig?"

Craig turned back to Jerry and continued to smile. "Wouldn't you like to know?"

"Come on, Craig." Jerry was frustrated. Not only was Craig not getting overwhelmed about the responsibilities of dog ownership, he was taking pleasure in Jerry's desire to get the dog away from him.

"You don't love dogs," Jerry continued. "She'll be a pain to take care of."

"Well, if you think it's a pain to take care of such a sweet little poochie," Craig said, obviously having a good time, "then you shouldn't own one." He laughed and headed off down the hall.

Jerry felt a wave of anxiety as he watched Craig disappear into a crowd of students. Getting the pup back from Craig was going to be a lot harder than he'd thought.

Chapter Five

"You guys!" Cinnamon burst into the classroom, beaming. "I want you two to know that the flirting worked! I *talked* to Sandy Powers. I actually had a *conversation* with him. *Twice.* See, Brenda? You just have to know how to go about it."

She plopped into an empty seat across from Jerry in the language arts room. "He's. So. Cool."

"Yeah, we saw you flirting yesterday and again just now," Brenda said, turning in her seat to face Cinnamon. "What do you two have in common?"

"Oh, who *knows?*" she said in a rush. "Who *cares?* He's so gorgeous, and he seems to *like* me. I got strong vibes about that. He definitely thinks I'm cute."

Jerry grinned. "Sounds to me like the basis for a lasting relationship."

Brenda laughed.

"That's exactly what *I* thought!" Cinnamon cried. She lowered her voice and leaned toward Jerry. "I know this sounds really, really dorky—and believe me, I'll never say this to Zoey—but I think I'm in love."

"That's great, Cinnamon," Jerry said. "I'm glad for you."

"Thanks," Cinnamon said. She turned to Brenda. "Let that be a lesson for you, Brenda. No one's ever estimated the power of a girl who knows how to flirt."

Brenda stared at her. "You mean, *under*estimated?"

"Whatever."

"I'll try to remember that."

"I *know* you can learn to flirt, Brenda. Here's a hot tip: practice in front of a mirror. It can really, really help. Big-time." Cinnamon reached over and patted Brenda on the shoulder, started to go to her seat, but rushed back.

"Oh, I almost forgot!" She lowered her voice again. "I even introduced Sandy to Zoey before school. It never hurts to let a guy know that you're friends with like the coolest girl in school." She winked knowingly at Brenda. "You're known by the company you keep. I could tell he thought Zoey was totally cool. Hey, Zoey happened to mention some really cool girl. Do you guys know somebody named Elena?"

"Yeah," Jerry said. "Elena Charles. She's in our class."

"I'm gonna have to get a look at that girl," Cinnamon said. "Zoey says she's cool, and if *Zoey* thinks she's cool, she's got to be *amazing*. See ya."

She scampered to her seat.

Brenda leaned over to Jerry and whispered, "Sounds like Zoey's doing a good job on this project for Elena."

"Sure does."

Gabe walked into the classroom and loped to his desk in the back. "Hey, Zoey."

Jerry turned to see Gabe leaning across his desk toward Zoey, who sat halfway across the room. She sat slumped in her seat, her arms folded across her chest. She turned her head and gave him a long, bored gaze.

"That girl you were talking to before school?" Gabe said.

"Yeah?"

"What's her name?" Gabe asked.

"Elena Charles. She's very cool."

Gabe's eyebrows lifted. "Yeah? I've seen her around. You friends with her?"

Zoey aimed a withering stare at him. "I just told you she's cool, didn't I?"

Cinnamon rolled her eyes. "In other words, Gabe, Zoey's only friends with cool people. Didn't you know that?"

"Hmm." Gabe sat back in his seat looking thoughtful.

Zoey faced the front and gave Jerry a barely perceptible nod. Jerry grinned back at her. One conversation with Zoey, and Gabe was asking about Elena. And he'd been mean to her up until this morning.

Amazing, Jerry thought. Zoey is *powerful.*

Ms. Robertson glanced at the clock. "Okay, we have just five minutes left on our *Midsummer Night's Dream* group discussion. How're you doing?"

Ms. R. had organized the class into small groups of six students to discuss questions she had passed out about the play.

"Jerry, is your group almost finished?"

"Yeah," he said. "We just have two more questions."

"Go ahead and finish, everyone."

Jerry gazed at his paper and read the second to last question. "'Helena's in love with Demetrius, even though he treats her very badly. Find one of his lines that shows the reader how he feels about her.'" He looked around at his group, which consisted of Brenda, Cinnamon, Carrie, Gabe, and Robin. "Anybody?"

Cinnamon held her chin in her hand, her elbow resting on the desk. She looked bored but spoke up. "Helena's totally stupid. That guy hates her and isn't even nice."

"We're supposed to find a line of his that shows that," Jerry said, glancing at his paper.

Cinnamon ignored him. "But it would be so *embarrassing* to throw yourself at a guy like that. Didn't she call herself his *spaniel?* Geez, she might as well lie down and say, 'Walk all over me' or something."

"Gabe?" Jerry said. Gabe hadn't said a word during the discussion. "We have to find a line from Demetrius that says how he feels about Helena."

Gabe was slumped in his seat with his legs stretched out in front of him. He didn't even glance at his book but looked up lazily. "I can't find one."

Brenda rolled her eyes at Gabe's comment. "How about this one? *'For I am sick when I do look on thee.'* I'd say he's making it pretty clear."

"Okay, that's good," Jerry said, writing on the paper. "And here's the last question. 'What does Helena say about love in her monologue in the first act? It has to do with how we see the people we love.'"

Brenda and Carrie began paging through their copies of the play. Cinnamon and Gabe stared off into space.

"Maybe this is it," Carrie said, pointing to a line.

"Helena says, *'Love looks not with the eyes, but with the mind.'*"

Cinnamon screwed up her face. "What does that mean?"

Carrie said, "She thinks that guys don't pay attention to what a girl looks like."

Cinnamon snorted. "Yeah, *right.*"

Jerry wrote Helena's line on the paper.

Ms. R. held up her hand to get attention. "Okay. Pass your papers forward. And one more thing before class is over for today. I talked with Jerry about this just before class, and he and his committee have come up with a good idea to help raise money for computers in the cafeteria.

"At the end of the unit, in two weeks, we're going to put on our own Elizabethan Festival in the gym."

Brenda turned to grin at Jerry. Their first project for the sixth grade was under way.

Ms. Robertson went on. "Any sixth grader who's participated in the after-school classes can take part in the festival. Your parents and friends will be invited, and you'll demonstrate what you've learned during our study of this time in history. We'll even wear simple costumes."

The bell rang. "Okay, we'll continue discussing tomorrow." She looked at Jerry. "May I talk to you?"

"Meet you in the hall," Brenda whispered.

"Right."

He hung back, wondering what Ms. R. wanted,

and waited for the classroom to empty.

"Jerry," she said, when the last of the students had filed out, "I think it'd be great if you'd say a few words to greet the visitors at the festival."

"You mean, while they walk in?" he asked.

"No," she said, sitting on the edge of her desk. "I'd like you to open the evening and make a few comments about our Elizabethan unit."

Jerry's heart sank. *Another speech in front of a huge crowd of people.* Just like his campaign speech less than two weeks ago.

"Really?" he asked.

"You're president of the sixth grade," Ms. Robertson said. She smiled. "And you'll do a good job."

Jerry felt a frown creasing his forehead, but he tried to force a smile. "Well—" His brain was running wildly in place, trying to think of a reason why he couldn't do it.

Ms. Robertson seemed to read his thoughts. Her smile widened. "You'll get used to speaking in public if you do it enough."

But Jerry didn't want to get used to it. He wanted to make the sixth grade the best it could be, but he wanted to do it from the background, not center stage.

Ms. Robertson watched him expectantly, waiting for his answer.

"It doesn't have to be very long," she said. "Really. Just a few minutes."

But a few minutes can feel interminable if you're scared to death, he thought. But he couldn't think of a way to get out of it.

"Okay."

"Wonderful! I can always depend on you, Jerry. Thank you."

"Sure." Even to him, his voice sounded very far away.

Jerry shuffled out of the classroom. Good old dependable Jerry, he thought. Roped into another speech. He'd thought the Elizabethan festival was going to be fun. But now, every time he'd think of it, he'd feel butterflies practicing their own stage combat for that night.

He sighed and held his hand up to greet Brenda who was waiting for him in the hall.

Jerry caught up with Zoey at the water fountain. "Hey, Zoey. You really scored big when Gabe asked about Elena. And all you did was *talk* to her."

Zoey nodded. "For an idiot, Gabe has decent taste. Elena's cool under that dorky exterior."

"So have you given her any tips yet on expressing her coolness?"

"I told her to lose the headband and try her hair in a ponytail," Zoey said. She shrugged. "First step."

"Great job," Jerry said. He glanced over Zoey's shoulder down the hall and expelled a laugh. "Guess who's already put her hair in a ponytail."

Elena Charles strode down the hall on long legs, her ponytail swinging. She watched the floor in front of her, but a couple of times glanced up self-consciously to see where she was going.

"It's a great first step," Jerry said.

Zoey smiled a little, nodded, and drifted off down the hall.

Jerry and Brenda stood back and watched as Jonathan Le Claire, dressed in sweats and sneakers, started the stage combat class that day after school. Ms. Robertson stood off to the side.

Jerry wasn't at all sure that this was his kind of class, but he was curious about it.

Twenty-three students had shown up at the south end of the gym for stage combat class. The floor under the basketball hoop was covered with mats. At the other end of the gym, instructors were teaching students how to juggle and how to build and perform with hand puppets. In different rooms scattered around the school, students were learning about performing magic tricks, madrigal singing, Elizabethan clothing and cooking, and some were building a miniature model of Shakespeare's Globe Theater. Jerry and Brenda had decided that, as organizers of the festival, they should sample classes to get a good overview.

Jerry wasn't surprised to see Gabe at this class. But he'd been amazed when Elena and Zoey walked in. Neither seemed the stage combat type—but then *he* was here, and he certainly wasn't the type, either.

Gabe had noticed Elena's and Zoey's entrance, too.

The last person to stroll in was Craig Fox. He walked over to Gabe and punched him in the arm. Gabe ignored him and fixed his eyes on Elena.

Jonathan was talking. "Stage combat is like sleight of hand," he said, looking at the students who gathered around him on three sides. "You don't really fight another actor. Instead, you work *with* your actor partner to perform the *illusion* of fighting. But, of course, no one's getting hurt. Safety is paramount. You protect yourself and your partner every second."

Jonathan looked around. "Okay, I need a volunteer to demonstrate."

Jerry was astonished when Zoey took a step forward. Students murmured, and Craig gave a loud whoop. Jerry gave Brenda a surprised glance, and she raised her eyebrows in response.

"Great," Jonathan said. "What's your name?"

"Zoey."

"Thanks for helping, Zoey." Jonathan turned back to the crowd of students.

"Okay, I'm going to show you what looks like a punch," Jonathan said. "But instead of punching straight into Zoey's face, my fist will move past it at an angle. I won't even touch her, but from where the audience is sitting, they won't be able to see that.

"First we set it up. Every bit of stage combat starts with the setup; it creates expectation," Jonathan continued. "You want your audience to expect this punch, to see it and hear it, and to watch the victim get hit and react. So here's the setup."

He maneuvered Zoey so her right side was to the students. "I pull my right arm back and make a fist. Now the audience is ready to see the punch. So I take a step forward, but I don't punch Zoey straight on; my fist moves past her like this."

He demonstrated by driving his fist from the side, just past Zoey's face. But a loud smack was heard, and Zoey cried out, her head jerked back, and she raised her hand to her face where he'd nearly punched her. She staggered backward, toppled over, and rolled onto her side, moaning.

The students whooped and clapped, Craig danced around in a circle, saying, "Man, oh man," and a look of surprise lit Jonathan's face.

Ms. Robertson moved a few steps forward, her expression concerned.

"Zoey, where in the world did you learn to take a stage punch and fall like that?" Jonathan asked her, his eyes gleaming with respect. He gave her a hand up off the floor.

Zoey shrugged. "A friend in L.A. taught me."

Ms. Robertson smiled and murmured, "My goodness."

"You learned well; that was excellent." He grinned. "This is great; now I have an assistant for demonstrating. This class will be much easier to teach."

Gabe spoke up. "If you didn't hit her, what made the sound of the slap?"

Jonathan replied, "Zoey did it. But she did it so fast—and you were watching me punch—that you didn't see it. Did you see her bring her hand up to her face, as if she were hurt? She smacked her hands together just before bringing her hand up and touching her face. She did it well. Come on, Zoey, let's show them again."

Jonathan and Zoey demonstrated four more times, breaking it down, so everyone saw each part of the punch and Zoey's response. "It's very important that you and your partner meet eyes, so you both know what's happening," Jonathan said. "Then the person throwing the punch must look where his or her fist is going. Remember, you're working *together*. Safety is first. Theatricality is second."

Jonathan stood with his hands on his hips and looked out at the students.

"Before we try the punch, let's concentrate on the fall. It's natural when you fall to catch yourself with a rigid arm. But that can cause injury, so we're going to learn what to do so that catching yourself like that isn't necessary.

"Control is essential here," Jonathan continued. "You're going to work against gravity; you don't want gravity to increase your impact with the floor. So you'll take a step back with your right leg. The muscles in your right thigh will control the fall." He turned to Zoey. "Show them slowly, Zoey. You'll counterbalance your weight by leaning forward as you lower yourself onto your right buttock and thrust your left leg forward on the floor. See how she did it? You should land smoothly. When your backside is completely on the floor, you twist to the left and hit the floor with your hands to increase the sound of impact, then extend your left arm under your head to ensure that you don't smack your head on the floor."

Zoey made it look easy. Jerry decided he could do it.

"Okay," Jonathan said. "Everyone get with a partner and watch each other as you try it. Zoey and I will circulate."

"Hey, Marshall!" Craig called out from his place next to the wall. "I wanna see you get punched out."

"Get lost, Fox," Gabe muttered. He looked self-conscious, and Jerry saw him glance at Elena to see if she was watching.

Craig laughed, but Jerry thought he saw a flash of hurt in his eyes.

Gabe walked over to Tony, who nodded. They would work as partners.

"Come on," Brenda said, nudging Jerry. "Let's practice the fall. When we get to the punch, I'll be the puncher first."

Jerry held up a hand. "Hey, remember, we're not fighting; we're working *together.*"

"I remember," she said, grinning. "But if we practice enough, we can fool people and make them think I'm punching you out."

Jerry laughed. "Great. That's just what I need to add to my reputation. A guy whose girlfriend likes to take punches at him."

Chapter Six

Jerry nudged Brenda after the stage combat class and said in a low voice, "Let's follow Craig."

Brenda's eyes widened. "Yeah. Maybe he'll show us where he's hidden the puppy."

Craig had watched for the entire class hour, not participating but hovering near Gabe, watching and taunting him with sarcastic comments.

As students gathered up their things, Gabe kept his eye on Elena; he walked out after her. Craig scurried along beside Gabe, talking and laughing, but Gabe didn't seem to be listening.

"Hurry and get your coat," Jerry said to Brenda. "I'll try and stall Craig at the locker."

"I'll be right there."

Jerry went to his locker, but Craig didn't come. He must have stopped at Gabe's locker, Jerry figured. He pulled out the notebooks he'd need tonight, along with his copy of *A Midsummer Night's Dream,* and shrugged into his jacket. He walked down the hall, around the corner, and stopped.

Craig and Gabe stood at Gabe's locker. Craig was talking and fooling around, but Gabe ignored him.

Jerry pretended to check his watch, even though he'd forgotten to put it on today and even though there was a huge clock hanging on the wall just above him. He glanced down the hall again.

Craig spoke up louder. "Wanna stop at the Corner Market and get a soda?" he asked Gabe.

Gabe apparently didn't hear Craig. He put on his jacket with a blank expression.

"Hey!" Craig called out in a loud voice. "*Gabe.*" He planted himself between Gabe and his locker. "Marshall, I'm talkin' to you."

Gabe pushed him out of the way. "I'm *busy,* Fox. I'll talk to you later." He trudged down the hall, away from Craig, who stood still, watching Gabe's back.

Brenda appeared, hurrying down the hall, and Jerry waved her over.

"Wait and see where Craig goes," he mumbled. "Pretend we're talking."

She smiled. "We *are* talking."

"You know what I mean."

Craig abruptly turned around and headed toward a side door.

"He isn't stopping at his locker," she whispered.

"It's warm, so he doesn't need a jacket," Jerry said. "And he never takes work home." They hung back a safe distance and then followed him out of the building and across the street.

"I looked up his address last night," Brenda said. "He lives on Mooney Drive."

Jerry nodded. "He's heading in that direction." He put a hand on her arm. "Let's slow down a bit. If he sees us behind him, he won't go to the pup."

"*If* he's going there now." She gritted her teeth. "He'd better be feeding that sweet little puppy."

They let Craig get nearly a block ahead of them and followed for five blocks. He never turned around. He also didn't look for traffic when he crossed streets, and twice a car skidded to a halt and honked at him.

"What's with him?" Brenda wondered aloud.

"I think he's mad," Jerry said. "Did you hear all the sarcastic comments he hollered at Gabe during combat class?"

"Yeah. Gabe totally ignored him. I think he was watching Elena."

"And that seemed to antagonize Craig. Did you see him? He started pacing and cracking his knuckles."

"I heard the knuckle cracking, even over the noise in the gym."

"I was thinking about that," Jerry said. "Craig really doesn't have friends, except for Gabe. When he's with Gabe, he hangs out with the popular guys."

"That's true," Brenda said. She sighed. "I just hope that Craig isn't so mad about Gabe ignoring him that he forgets to take care of the puppy."

"I know."

Up ahead, Craig turned into a yard behind a small gray house. He walked across the grass to the door of an old shed.

Jerry and Brenda reached the yard and stopped behind a scraggly lilac bush.

Craig fished something out of his pocket and unlocked a padlock on the door.

Soft whimpers came from inside.

"He's keeping her locked inside that old shed!" Brenda cried. Rage blazed in her eyes. "He's *not* taking care of her! Let's go get her."

"I'm with you," Jerry said, and they headed toward the shed.

His heart was beating hard. The puppy didn't belong to Craig, and he certainly wasn't giving her good care if he'd locked her in the shed all day.

They reached the shed door and looked inside.

"That dog doesn't belong to you, Craig," Jerry said in his most forceful voice.

Craig was kneeling on the dirt floor of the shed, scratching the puppy's head. The pup wiggled all over and licked his hand.

Brenda pushed forward and scooped up the puppy. "You aren't even feeding her!" she raged. "She's so skinny, she must be starving to death!"

"Give her back!" Craig yelled. He tried to pull the pup out of Brenda's arms, but Jerry pushed him out of the way.

"We're taking her, Craig, because she was never your dog. I know that because I called your house last night, and your dad said you don't *have* a—"

He was interrupted by a big voice behind him.

"What's going on here?"

Jerry whirled around to see a man—he figured it was Craig's father—lumber across the yard. The man wasn't tall, but he was broad across the chest, like a wrestler, and had a neck the size of a small tree trunk. His face was ruddy and crisscrossed with scars; he looked angry.

Jerry swallowed. "This dog doesn't belong to Craig," he said. "We want to give her a good home."

The man scowled at Craig. "You been keeping this mutt out here?" he said.

"Yeah," Craig said in a small voice.

"Where'd you get it?"

"I found it," Craig answered.

"So why are they trying to take it away from you?"

"Mr. Fox," Jerry spoke up. "This puppy was a stray. We found her first."

"That's a lie!" Craig cried.

"No, we're telling you the truth," Jerry said. "She's very thin, as you can see. We just want to take care of her. She's been locked up in this shed all day."

"Well, you're not going to take away my kid's dog," Craig's dad said. His eyes shifted to Brenda. "Hand it over. If he found it, he can have it."

"But *we* found her first," Brenda said, tears brimming in her eyes. "Please, Mr. Fox. She'll get sick and die if she doesn't get more food and fresh air." The puppy whimpered and licked her chin.

Craig's dad's voice got louder. "*I said, hand it over.*"

Brenda gently put the puppy in Craig's arms as a tear splashed down her cheek.

"He'll feed it," Mr. Fox said. "Now go on—you kids get out of here." He pulled a few dollars from his pocket and shoved them at Craig. "Get some food, but you keep it out here in the shed, you hear?"

Jerry put his arm around Brenda's shoulder and led her out of the yard. He was shaking, he was so angry.

Brenda was crying hard as they reached the sidewalk. She sniffed. "Why would Craig's dad stand up for him? He obviously doesn't even like dogs."

"I don't think it had anything to do with the pup," Jerry said. "He was standing up for Craig."

Jerry's heart felt squeezed tight inside his chest.

Brenda pulled a tissue out of her pocket. "It's not fair," she said, wiping her nose. "Craig had locked her in that shed all day, but she's so starved for love, she was licking his hand." Brenda's face was covered with red blotches from crying.

Impulsively, Jerry leaned over and kissed her cheek. He tasted salt from her tears. "I'll figure out something," he said. "I don't know how, but we'll get her back."

We have to, he thought. *The pup's life probably depends on it.*

"We've decided on the play we want to do," Melissa said.

Melissa and Jerry were surrounded by nine first graders. They'd met in the Flacks' basement to start working on the play they would perform for their class in less than two weeks.

"Good," Jerry said. "What's the name of the play?"

"It's called *Camouflage Girl.*"

Jerry nodded. "You found this play at the library?"

Melissa blew out an exasperated breath that lifted her bangs a moment. "No, Jerry! We *made it up*! Actually, *I* made it up, but Rachel helped a little."

"Actually, it was kind of a lot," Rachel murmured. She stood next to Melissa and gazed up at Jerry with an earnest light in her eyes. "It's a really great play."

Three of the girls stayed near Melissa and Rachel, but the rest scampered off to the far end of the basement. One of the girls had a rubber ball, and she began throwing it at the others, who shrieked and ran away.

"Have you written the play?" Jerry asked. One of the girls ran past him, screeching. The rest of the girls laughed. Jerry leaned closer to talk to Melissa. "I want to read it."

"No," Melissa said, rolling her eyes. "We didn't write it down. It's easier just to make it up as we go. But we figured out the story."

It sounded like a disorganized way of putting on a play, he thought. But it was their project.

"Okay," he said.

"It's about this fairy named Snowflake," Melissa said. "She wants to be a human being, so she goes to school and pretends to be human. That's where the title comes from. See, she's *camouflaging* herself. Get it?"

The five girls at the other side of the basement all screamed and laughed at one time, hurting Jerry's ears.

"Sure. So what happens?" Jerry asked, raising his voice over the din. "Does she convince everyone that she's a human being?"

"Yeah, for a while, but she gets in trouble, 'cause she lies all the time about stuff. At the end, she decides she'd rather be herself and flit around over people's heads and throw fairy dust at them and make them fly, like in *Peter Pan,* and shoot them with arrows, so they fall in love and stuff."

"I think you're confusing her with Cupid," Jerry said.

"Whatever. I'm the writer, so I get to decide what she can do. I also think I should play the part of the girl."

"Melissa, you're the playwright, so maybe you should help me direct."

"No, I can play a good fairy," Melissa insisted. "I'll throw fake fairy dust—you know, like glitter— and make the most popular girl in school fall in love with the class dork. The kids in my class will love it. They'll laugh their heads off. So will Mrs. Loonybin."

Jerry frowned. "Your teacher's name is Mrs. Loonybin?"

"No, it's really Mrs. Loney, but she's really funny, so we call her Mrs. Loonybin. Not to her face, though."

"Smart move," Jerry said. "So what about the rest of the girls? What parts will they play?"

"They can be the kids at school," Melissa said. She shrugged. "Or whatever."

Jerry had serious doubts that this play would

work. It was a silly idea, pure fluff. Who would be interested in a story like that? On the other hand, he didn't have time to read plays at the library to find a story that had more substance.

"Okay, Missy," he said. "We'll do your play, *Girl in Camouflage.*"

"No! *Camouflage Girl!*"

"Okay, right."

Melissa jumped. "Yay! This will be the best play anybody's ever seen!"

"Gather 'round, everyone," Jerry called out. "Let's get to work."

Chapter Seven

When Jerry arrived at school the next day, he spotted Zoey standing with Elena and strolled over to them. Elena was wearing her hair in a ponytail again, and she leaned in to talk to Zoey.

"Do you know Gabe Marshall?" Elena murmured.

"Yeah," Zoey said.

"What do you think of him?" Elena asked. "He's been kind of a jerk around me, but I can't stop thinking about—" She looked up, startled. Her cheeks colored, and her hand flew up to cover her mouth. "Oh, hi, Jerry. I didn't see you there."

"You want to know what *I* think of Gabe Marshall?" Jerry asked, smiling.

"I think I already know. I saw what he did to you during the election."

"I think you could do a whole lot better," Jerry said.

Elena smiled and looked at the sidewalk. "Thanks. Zoey's been giving me some pointers about being cool. I'm not naturally too cool, in case you hadn't noticed."

"If anyone can teach you cool," Jerry said, "it's Zoey."

Elena turned to Zoey. "I interrupted you to ask about Gabe. What were you saying about my pants?" She glanced at her brown cotton pants.

"You got jeans?" Zoey asked. Elena nodded. "Let's see you wear them to school."

"Okay."

Just then, Sandy Powers appeared at Zoey's side. "Hey, Zoe," he said. "What's up?"

Zoey nodded at him and said to Elena, "This is Sandy Powers. He goes with Cinnamon O'Brien."

Elena nodded. "I know who Cinnamon is."

Zoey said to Sandy, "This is Elena."

Sandy's eyes lit up. "Oooh, yeah. Zoey mentioned you yesterday." He flashed her a dazzling smile. "Hi."

"Hello," she answered.

"Uh, I'm Jerry Flack," Jerry said to Sandy.

"Hi," Sandy said. But he was still smiling at Elena.

"Well, I have to go over my science notes before the test," Elena said. "See you." She disappeared into a crowd of students.

"A very cool girl," Sandy said, his head bobbing up and down. He turned to Zoey. "You were right."

Jerry wasn't sure how Sandy could tell Elena was cool after just exchanging a few words with her. But it was Zoey's magic at work again. Jerry was amazed. If Zoey could only bottle that stuff, he thought, she'd win a Nobel Prize for sure.

Ms. Robertson looked up from her copy of *A Midsummer Night's Dream*. "Here we meet the amateur actors in the forest, preparing to rehearse a play for the duke's wedding," she said. "Did you like Nick Bottom? He's probably Shakespeare's most famous comedy character."

Brenda spoke up. "He's got a big ego."

"How so?"

"He wants to run everything, including acting the parts of *both* the male and female lead. *And* the lion."

Ms. R. smiled. "Somebody find a few of Bottom's lines that demonstrate his boastfulness."

"I got it," said Josh Bailey. "He's talking about playing the lion.

"I grant you, friends, if you should fright the ladies out of their wits, they would have no

more discretion but to hang us; but I will aggravate my voice so that I will roar you as gently as any sucking dove; I will roar you an 'twere any nightingale.'

"You think Bottom should worry about scaring the ladies?" Ms. R. asked.

"No, they'll think he's stupid," Robin answered.

Jerry was hearing his little sister's voice in his head. She was trying to convince Jerry to let her play the fairy in the play she wrote. *"I can play a good fairy,"* Melissa had said. *"The kids in my class will love it. They'll laugh their heads off. So will Mrs. Loonybin."*

Jerry sighed. His little sister was some piece of work, all right. Sometimes real life had a way of being as goofy as a comedy onstage.

"Hey, Gabe!" Craig yelled. The sixth graders were lining up to get lunch. Craig stood at the front of the line; Gabe was nearly at the end. "Come up here! You can cut in."

"I hate people cutting in," Brenda muttered.

"Me, too," Jerry agreed.

They turned with dozens of students to give Gabe the evil eye for cutting in front of everyone else. Gabe didn't seem to notice; he loped toward the front of the line. But about five yards from Craig, he turned his head and stopped.

"Uh, no, I'll wait back here," Gabe said. He turned away.

"*Come on, Marshall!*" Craig called.

Gabe shook his head and walked to the end of the line.

"He's not cutting?" Brenda murmured. "What happened?"

"He saw Elena," Jerry said.

"You're kidding. That stopped him?"

"Well, cutting in line makes people mad, and he doesn't want to look bad in front of Elena."

"Wow," Brenda said. "Interesting."

"It sure is."

Craig seemed at a loss when Gabe didn't join him at the front of the line. He stood there, absent-mindedly pulling on his ear.

He looked over and saw Jerry. "Hey, Flack!" he yelled.

Jerry raised his head.

"You still want the dog?"

Jerry's heart quickened. He heard Brenda take in a breath; she squeezed his arm.

"Sure, we want the dog," he called out.

"I'll let ya have it on one condition!"

Jerry didn't like the grin on his face; it definitely wasn't a good sign. He was aware that all the kids in line had turned to listen.

"What condition?" Jerry asked.

"You have to eat *dog food* tomorrow for lunch!"

"What?"

Craig laughed. "You heard me."

A girl in front of him turned around and grinned. "He said you have to eat dog food for lunch tomorrow."

Jerry felt all eyes on him. "Jerry. . ." Brenda whispered. "We can save her!"

He swallowed. *Dog food?* His stomach lurched.

"Yeah," Craig yelled at him. "To prove you're worthy." He was still grinning, obviously loving the limelight. "Tomorrow at lunch. I'll bring the can of food. Take it or leave it."

Brenda squeezed his arm again. Jerry took a big breath. "Okay," he said. "I'll take it."

Craig whooped. "*All right!* This is gonna be *so cool!*"

Some of the students murmured and laughed.

"You're going to eat dog food tomorrow?" Robin asked.

Nate Thompsen made a face. "To get a dog? Why don't you just go to the humane shelter? It'd be easier."

Brenda stepped close to Jerry and whispered in his ear, "*Oh, thank you, Jerry. Thank you!*"

Several important questions were looming in Jerry's brain. Did he have to eat a *whole* can of dog food? He wondered who would make a ruling on that. Who would decide when he had eaten enough and earned the right to have the pup?

"This is going to be so fun!" Craig chortled.

Of course, Jerry knew the answer to his questions. That was easy.

Craig had the upper hand. He had the dog.

Craig would decide.

Jerry wondered what it would be like tomorrow. What, exactly, does dog food taste like? He'd given his dog, Sassy, food from a can many times. It smelled horrible.

Oh, boy, he thought. Dog food for lunch. Could he really eat it? And more important, could he keep it down?

Chapter Eight

"The Globe Theater is where many of William Shakespeare's plays were first performed," said Mr. Dingleberry, the art teacher. "Our miniature replica of the Globe will be on display at the Elizabethan Festival."

Jerry and Brenda had decided to visit this class after school. Only ten students had elected to take this one. They gathered around a table in the middle of the room. On the table was a large piece of quarter-inch plywood that would be the model's base. The students had already drawn on the board indicating where the stage was located at one side of an open courtyard, inside the theater walls. Several books about the Globe Theater lay open on the table for reference.

"Is this where the people sat to watch the plays?" Brenda asked, pointing to the courtyard in front of the stage.

"Yes they watched the play from there," Mr. Dingleberry said, "but they stood. As many as three thousand people could crowd into the courtyard and watch the plays."

"Three thousand!" Jerry said. "That's like a rock concert."

Mr. Dingleberry gestured at the area drawn on the board. "Rich people sat in the more expensive seats in the balconies that surrounded the courtyard. People brought their own food and drink to consume while they watched the play. Drinking water wasn't chemically treated as it is today, so it wasn't safe. So people drank ale instead. They frequently got tipsy at the theater, and if they didn't like the play, they'd yell at the actors and throw food at them."

Brenda laughed. "How'd you like to be an actor back then? And get hit in the head with an apple core. I'd want to throw it back at the audience."

"Well, you wouldn't be onstage in the first place," Mr. Dingleberry said. "Girls weren't allowed to be actors."

"Why not?"

"It wasn't considered a proper thing for ladies to do," he said.

"So who played the women's parts?" Jerry asked.

"The female parts were played by young boys whose voices hadn't changed yet," Mr. Dingleberry said.

"Well, that's not fair," Brenda said.

"A lot of the plays had violence in them. So acting was considered to be a rough profession." Mr. Dingleberry looked around. "Okay, we've got the areas marked on the board. Now let's start building the theater. We'll draw it first on cardboard, and then cut it out. I have the cardboard in the cabinet." He left to get it.

Todd Newman leaned over to Jerry. "I keep thinking about you eating dog food tomorrow. You're not really going through with it, are you?"

Jerry felt his stomach lurch again. He hadn't thought about the dog food for a full five minutes, and he didn't want to think or talk about it now.

"Yeah," Jerry said. He was aware that the other students were listening to the conversation.

Todd winced. "But why?"

"To save a dog," Jerry answered.

Todd blew out a breath and shook his head. "I wouldn't do it for anything."

"Me either," echoed Sarah Johnson. "I'd barf if I had to eat dog food."

"Well, maybe I'd do it to save my life," Austin Perkins said, "but not to save a dog." He thought a moment, then added, "Or my sister."

Brenda put a hand on Jerry's arm. "Well, I'm sure glad Jerry's willing to do it to save a dog."

Jerry gulped. He just hoped he could go through with it when the time came.

That night, Jerry went to the pantry and pulled out a can of dog food. Sassy jumped up and barked, knowing she was about to be fed. Her claws clicked on the vinyl floor as she danced around his legs.

"Hold on, girl," he told her. "It's coming."

Jerry positioned the can next to the can opener and pushed the lever to turn it on. The smell of the dog food wafted past Jerry's nose, and he winced. It was *awful*. It smelled like meat, but not the way his mother made it, laced with garlic and spices and Worcestershire sauce. Instead, it smelled dirty, the way he imagined the inside of a slaughterhouse would smell.

"I don't know what you see in this stuff," he said to Sassy, who barked for him to hurry.

Jerry took off the can lid, rinsed it, and tossed it in the recycling bag under the sink. He pulled a spoon out of the drawer and scooped out some of the slimy dog food. As usual, he held his breath and plopped it into Sassy's bowl.

He pictured in his mind the pup in Craig's back-yard shack, begging for love and licking Craig's hand, so happy to see him. She was probably happy to see *anybody* after spending the whole day locked inside a small, musty old shack. Jerry had to keep the pup foremost in his mind if he was going to eat the dog food tomorrow. He had to remember why it was so important for him to go through with such a disgusting act.

If he could just gag down the dog food, Brenda would be able to take the pup home and give her a clean, loving place to live with plenty of good food.

Sassy barked with impatience again, and he put the food on the floor. "There you go, Sass," he said.

She dove at the bowl, eating with relish, her license clanking against the stainless steel.

"Whoo, boy," he murmured.

His mother walked into the kitchen. "What did you say?" she asked.

"Uh, nothing," Jerry said. "I'm going up to do homework."

"Okay."

Jerry fled upstairs to his room where he could think about Shakespeare or science or anything that wasn't related to the sickening stench of dog food.

"Let's get up to date on *A Midsummer Night's Dream*," Ms. Robertson said, looking out over the students. "Let's talk about what's happening with our four protagonists." She leaned against her desk and turned a page in her book. "Turn to the scene where Oberon asks Puck to use nectar from a magic flower to make Demetrius fall in love with Helena. Jerry, will you read those lines?"

Jerry found his place in the play and read:

> *"Take thou some of it, and seek through this*
> *grove.*
> *A sweet Athenian lady is in love*
> *With a disdainful youth: anoint his eyes,*
> *But do it when the next thing he espies*
> *May be the lady."*

"So," Ms. Robertson said, "does Puck's love potion work?" She gazed at the back of the room. "Gabe?"

Silence filled the room, followed by a few soft snickers from Gabe's friends.

"Gabe, did you read the scenes I assigned for today?"

"Yeah," Gabe said. "I was just looking for the page."

Brenda turned back and raised her eyebrows at Jerry. Jerry was surprised that Gabe had actually read it, too. At least, he *said* he'd read it. He rarely did the assigned homework and usually seemed proud of it.

"Well," Gabe said, "Puck makes a mistake and puts the magic stuff on the wrong guy. He puts it on Lysander's eyes."

"Yes," Ms. R. said, her eyes wide and staring at Gabe. There was no mistaking the astonishment on her face. "Very good, Gabe." Small pockets of laughter were heard around the room. "And what happens when Lysander wakes up?"

"He sees Helena first and falls for her," Gabe said.

"He really read it," Brenda whispered to Jerry.

"That's right," Ms. R. said, smiling at Gabe. "With nothing more than a little magic, Puck can make one person fall in love with someone else. This magic potion is an interesting way for the forest sprites to manipulate human beings. He has fun with it, too, doesn't he?"

Brenda turned around and grinned at Jerry.

Jerry smiled back and nodded at Brenda.

Yes, he thought. Using a little magic to influence people—especially Zoey's brand of magic—could really be fun.

After language arts class, Jerry and Brenda met up with Zoey in the hall.

"You going to eat dog food today?" Zoey asked him.

Although Jerry had tried not to think about dog food this morning, the subject was never far from his mind.

"I have to," Jerry said. He had a peculiar sensation in his stomach, as if something were curdling. "I have to get that dog away from Craig. He isn't taking care of her."

Zoey nodded thoughtfully. "Interesting hoop he chose."

"What?"

"For you to jump through."

"Oh. Yeah."

Brenda glanced over Jerry's shoulder. "Speaking of interesting."

Jerry turned to see ponytailed Elena, wearing jeans, walking down the hall. Sandy was hurrying to catch up with her.

"Hey, Elena," Sandy said to her.

Elena looked at him, surprised. "Oh. Hi."

"So, uh, you have your first period class around here?" Sandy asked.

Elena didn't seem to know what to make of the attention from this handsome seventh grader.

"Hey, Elena," Gabe said. He had suddenly appeared on the other side of her. "I've been meaning to ask you something."

Elena turned and frowned, fixing a suspicious gaze on him.

Sandy, Gabe, and Elena were all tall, nearly the same height. Gabe gave Sandy an annoyed look and stepped closer to Elena, who stepped back.

"What do you want?" she said to Gabe, eyeing him warily.

Gabe shrugged. "Uh, I just wanted to know if you're taking any of the other Elizabethan classes after school. I mean, other than stage combat?"

Sandy held out a stick of gum. "Want a Juicy Fruit?"

Elena blinked and looked back and forth at the two boys. "What's going on here?"

"What do you mean?" Gabe and Sandy asked in unison.

"Oh, I get it," Elena said. "This is some kind of trick, isn't it?"

"What are you talking about?" Sandy asked her.

Elena whirled to face him. "You think just because you're good-looking, you can have fun at someone else's expense."

Sandy tilted his head to one side, smiling a little, and the dimples in his cheeks deepened. "You think I'm good-looking?"

Elena turned on Gabe now. "And you! You played lots of tricks on Jerry Flack when he was running against you for sixth-grade president, and now you've decided to pick on me! I don't understand how people can think the way you do! What's *wrong* with you? You think it's okay to act like this just because you're the cutest guy in the sixth grade!"

Gabe grinned modestly. "Well, I wouldn't say the cutest. Maybe *one* of the cutest—"

"Oh, hi, Sandy!" Jerry heard Cinnamon's voice behind him. "What are you doing up here? Don't you have classes on the first floor in the mornings?"

"Oh-oh," Brenda whispered next to Jerry.

Sandy's head jerked up and his smile faded. "Oh, uh—hi."

"What's everybody doing here?" Cinnamon looked up at Elena. "Who are you?"

"Elena Charles," she said, still scowling.

"Ohhhhhh." Cinnamon stepped back and gave her a once-over. "I've heard about you."

Elena backed away. "Okay, that's it. You're all in this together! Well, you'd better stop right now! You'd better just *leave me alone*!"

She turned and strode down the hall, fury blazing in her eyes.

Cinnamon held up her hands. "What'd I do?"

Sandy and Gabe, obviously baffled, turned away from her, lost in their own thoughts, and they started off in different directions.

"Huh?" Cinnamon said. "What'd I *do*? Hey, Sandy—" She hurried to follow him down the hall.

"Wow," Brenda murmured. "This project to make people notice Elena is getting complicated."

"Yeah," Jerry said. He turned to Zoey. "You'll have to tell her you saw what happened and make sure she understands that they weren't making fun of her." He smiled. "But all this happened because of your awesome magical powers. Elena's suddenly very popular."

"Yeah," Brenda said. "Now Elena's liked by two of the most popular guys at school."

A small smile curled the edges of Zoey's lips.

"Cool," she said. She turned and drifted off down the hall.

Brenda stopped Jerry outside the cafeteria door and looked him in the eyes. "Are you ready?" she asked.

His heart fluttered, and his stomach was roiling like storm clouds, but he nodded. "As ready as I'll ever be, I guess."

They entered the cafeteria together. The whole sixth grade was waiting for him, standing and watching the doorway. When they spotted him, the air came alive with whispers.

"There he is!"

"He really came."

"Do you think he'll eat the dog food?"

"I can't believe he'd do that—*gross!*"

The whispers gradually diminished, and the cafeteria grew quiet. The students stood, waiting to see what Jerry would do.

Oh, geez, Jerry thought. *If I barf, the whole class will be watching.*

Craig stood next to Jerry's usual table, holding a can in his hand.

The dog food he was going to have to eat.

"Hello, Jerry," Craig said with a malevolent grin. He wiggled the can of dog food back and forth in front of him. "Come and eat your lunch."

Jerry took in a big breath and let it out. He

started slowly across the cafeteria, the crowds of students silently parting like the Red Sea to let him through. Jerry read many different things in the eyes of his classmates: concern, fright, nervousness. Nausea.

He stopped in front of his table.

He suddenly thought of something and glanced around the room. Wasn't there usually a teacher here to monitor the lunchroom? He probably wouldn't have to eat the dog food because the teacher on lunchroom duty would never allow it!

He was filled with hope.

"Someone suddenly felt sick and had to be taken to the nurse," Craig said, grinning, guessing his thoughts. "What luck. But you'll have to eat fast if you want the dog."

Did Craig make someone sick just to get the teacher out of the room? Maybe he'd just persuaded somebody to fake being sick. That's probably what had happened. Jerry saw Gabe watching from the crowd, so the faker wasn't Gabe. Craig would've wanted Gabe to be here to watch the spectacle.

"Come on, fearless leader," Craig said. He looked out over the crowd of students. "This'll be better than TV, watching our sixth-grade president eat dog food."

Craig picked up a can opener on the table and held it over his head for everyone to see and announced in a big voice, "I will now open the can of dog food."

He set the can in front of him on the table, hooked the opener over the edge, locked it, and cranked the key to open the can. Even from where he stood, Jerry could smell the stench of the dog food.

His stomach churned.

"Sit down, Jerry," Craig said, "and eat the lunch that I've spent all morning preparing." He laughed at his own joke and held up a spoon. "Dig in!"

Jerry took a deep breath and sat down at the table. He took the spoon from Craig. The students crowded in closer to watch. They were still quiet, waiting for him to start eating.

"Brenda, will you hold my nose, please?" Jerry asked, his voice shaking.

Jerry knew that smelling was an important element of taste. When he had a cold, he could hardly taste his food. Having his nose plugged would help.

He hoped.

Brenda sat down on his left side, probably knowing that he'd need his right hand to eat.

"Ready?" she asked.

He nodded.

She reached over and pinched his nostrils together.

Jerry stuck the spoon in the dog food and scooped out a little. It was a different brand than the food his family fed Sassy, but it looked just as slimy and disgusting.

"You know what dog food is made out of?" Craig asked, still smiling. "It's made out of the animal parts that people don't want to eat. Like the eyeballs and the brains and the tongues of cows and pigs and stuff."

Jerry wished he hadn't heard that. He wished he'd asked somebody to plug his ears, too. But it was too late.

He put the spoonful of eyeballs and brains into his mouth, and a cry of disgust went up from the crowd. He chewed and chewed and swallowed.

Think about the pup. Think about the pup. Think about the pup.

Those four words would be his mantra for the next five minutes. He wasn't eating dog food; he was saving a sweet little pup who needed a good, loving home. He wasn't eating dog food; he was helping his best, most loyal friend, Brenda, to get the pup she wanted for her very own.

He fed himself another spoonful, and the crowd groaned again.

"I can't believe he's doing it!" a girl shrieked.

"That's the most disgusting thing I've ever seen," a guy said.

"You're wonderful, Jerry," Brenda whispered. "You're the best, bravest, most generous friend I've ever had. Thank you, thank you, thank you. You're saving her life."

He was glad he'd asked Brenda to hold his nose.

It was awful, but the taste was surely fainter than it would have been if he could smell it, as well.

It's about the pup; I'm saving the pup; she'll be Brenda's at the end of the day.

It took nearly five minutes, but he finished the dog food in the can. He held it up to show it was empty, and a cheer went up from the crowd. Brenda released his nose and threw her arms around him.

And that's when he could smell again, and really taste the greasy stuff that was left in his mouth. He felt a heaving spasm in his stomach.

He jumped up from the table. At first, he had to push surprised students out of the way. But they caught on fast and hurried to give him a path.

He charged out of the cafeteria and around the corner to the boys' bathroom.

He just made it to the first stall before he got a second look at all that dog food.

Chapter Nine

When Jerry finally walked out of the boys' bathroom, a small crowd of sixth graders was standing in the hall, waiting for him. Brenda was at the front, smiling. Beside her were Zoey, Cinnamon, and the Henley sisters. Jerry also saw Elena near the back, and Gabe was standing off to one side.

"Yay, Jerry!" Brenda shouted, shoving her fist in the air. "You saved the puppy! Thank you! Thank you!"

Some of the kids cheered and applauded.

"You're wonderful," Brenda said, throwing her arms around him in a quick hug. "I don't know how to thank you."

Jerry shrugged and gave her a wan smile with his lips pressed together.

"That was a noble thing you did," Brenda said.

She looked at him carefully. "Are you okay?"

Jerry nodded.

"He's in shock after throwing up all that dog food," Cinnamon said with a giggle.

"He's so modest," Kat said.

Kim nodded. "Jerry never toots his own horn."

"He's a hero," Brenda added.

But it wasn't shock or modesty that was keeping his mouth closed. Or even the fact that his stomach was still feeling terrible.

It was his breath. Jerry was sure it was bad enough to kill an elephant. He didn't want to open his mouth and breathe on anyone.

"Hey." Craig elbowed his way to the front of the crowd. "Sorry, Flack," he said. "But it doesn't count if you throw up the dog food."

"*What!*" Brenda cried. "The whole deal was that Jerry had to *eat* the dog food! And he ate it in front of over a hundred witnesses! You can't back out of our agreement now!"

"But the idea of eating sort of means keeping it down."

"*It does not!*"

"Well," Craig said, "I have the dog, see, so I get to decide." He grinned maliciously. "He stays in the shed—"

"*SHE!*" Brenda cried fiercely. "Your dog is a *female*, Craig Fox!"

"Whatever," Craig said. "The dog stays in the

shed." A light came into his eyes. "Unless—" He turned, grinning, and put up his index finger.

Jerry's heart started beating hard again. What more could Craig ask him to do?

"Unless WHAT?" Brenda shouted at him.

Craig glanced over at Gabe to get his reaction. But Gabe didn't seem to be enjoying Craig's game. He didn't even seem to be paying much attention; he was gazing over the heads of the students at Elena.

"I heard you have to give a speech at that fair thing," Craig said.

Jerry nodded. The Elizabethan fair. Oh, geez, he'd almost forgotten about the speech.

"Jerry can have the dog at the fair, if—" Craig said, talking slowly to draw out the suspense.

"If WHAT?" Brenda shouted.

"If he gives the speech . . . wearing a dress."

Cinnamon shrieked with laughter. "Jerry? Wearing a *dress*? I can't even imagine that!"

Laughter ran through the crowd.

"I'll bring the dog to the fair," Craig said. "I'll turn it—I'll turn her—the *dog* over to Jerry right after his speech, if he's worn the dress while talking to the crowd." He shrugged. "How easy is that, Flack? You don't even have to put on the dress till you see me with the little doggie that you want *so much*."

"He can't do that!" Brenda cried. "Besides, he

already ate the dog food! The dog is mine now! You promised!"

"I don't think so, and I'm sure my dad wouldn't think so," Craig said.

"That's not fair!" Brenda roared. "Jerry won the dog fair and square."

Cinnamon giggled. "But it sure would be funny to see Jerry wearing a dress at the festival."

Some of the students laughed.

"And you say you'd bring the dog to the festival," Robin said to Craig. She was grinning, really enjoying this. "And you'd hand the dog over after Jerry's speech?"

Craig nodded emphatically. "Right after."

"Hey, Jerry! What a deal!" Robin laughed.

Jerry felt sick and depressed. He turned and trudged down the hall. He didn't want to think about the dog. He didn't want to think about dog food. And he certainly didn't want to think about giving a speech in front of a big crowd—wearing a *dress*.

That was going too far.

Jerry and Brenda didn't feel like going to an after-school class, so they headed for home at the end of the school day. They walked together in silence for three blocks.

Jerry had sipped a Coke at school and chewed gum between classes, so his stomach felt much better, and the taste of the dog food was gone from his mouth. But every time he looked at Brenda, his chest ached because she looked so sad.

"I thought we had the puppy," Brenda said finally. "I thought I'd be picking her up right now and taking her home."

"I'm sorry, Bren. I thought so, too. Maybe Craig never meant to turn her over to us."

"I don't know," Brenda said. "He doesn't act as if he cares about her at all. He can't even remember that she's a *female*."

"Maybe he just wants to see me dance," Jerry said. "Like in those old Western movies when the bad guy shoots at the feet of his victims and makes them jump and dance when they try to hop out of the way."

"Yeah," Brenda said. "Craig knows how much you care about the puppy. He's got you right where he wants you. He knows you'll do just about anything to get her."

"Except wear a dress," Jerry said. "I'm sorry, Bren, but there's no way—"

"Oh, of course not."

"Everyone will be there. My parents even want to come."

"Right," Brenda agreed. "Mine, too."

"I'm president of the sixth grade," Jerry continued. "I mean, everyone would think I'd lost my mind if I gave the welcoming speech in a dress."

"Yes, they would."

"I can't do it. It'd be too embarrassing. And who's to say Craig would really give up the puppy? He didn't this time."

"Right."

"Ms. Robertson would be horrified, my parents would be even more horrified, and I'd probably get suspended from school," Jerry said.

"Yeah."

He stopped and turned to her, his chest aching. "So why do I feel so guilty?"

Her eyes filled with tears. "Because it's the only way we know to save her. And you can't do it."

"I can't."

"No."

Jerry put his arms around Brenda and hugged her hard. He rested his hand on her hair. He stroked it gently; it felt silky and clean. He could feel her ragged breathing against him, and he knew she was crying.

"I'm sorry, Bren," he murmured.

"I know."

He knew that she knew he was sorry. So why didn't he feel any better?

The first graders sat cross-legged under the maple tree in the Flacks' backyard, looking up at Jerry. A warm autumn breeze sighed through the branches overhead and stirred the girls' hair.

He smiled and clapped his hands together. "Okay, are we ready to get to work on our play?" He looked around at the girls.

Two of them murmured, "Yes." The others just stared up at him.

"I have a question," Melissa said. "You know when some of the kids are mean to me because they don't think I'm a real human being?"

"Yeah."

"Well, what if that makes Mrs. Loonybin and the rest of the class mad? 'Cause teachers always want us to be nice, you know, and if the characters in the play are mean to me, she and the other kids might start yelling at the characters in the play to knock it off and be nice. Mrs. Loonybin might even tell the kids—the *actresses*—that they can't go out for recess."

"No, she won't, Melissa," Jerry said. "Your teacher will know that this is a play. She'll know you're playing characters, and it's just pretend."

"Well," Melissa said, "maybe I should make a speech just before the play to tell them that we're just pretending and that they shouldn't get upset."

"It's really not necessary, Missy," Jerry said.

"Well, *I* think it is," she said, getting to her feet. "And I don't want Mrs. Loonybin or the kids in the audience to feel too sorry for me when I'm a fairy pretending to be a real girl. I think I should explain before the play starts."

Jerry sighed. "Okay."

"I'll say something like this: 'Mrs. Loonybin—I mean, Mrs. Loney and kids, we want you to know'—wait. What about, 'To our favorite people: we thought we should explain'—no. Okay, I got it! Here it is: 'To our favorite teacher and kids in the class who are all very cool, we want to tell you before we begin that this is just a play.'" She gestured dramatically with her arms outstretched. "'Some of us are going to be playing characters who aren't very nice, but it isn't *us*, ya see? We're just pretending, because this is a play. And I'm not really a fairy. I'm an *actress*! We know, Mrs. Loney, that you're old and tired, and you deserve a rest after all your teaching. So sit back and enjoy the show.'" She looked at Jerry with a satisfied smile. "How's that?"

Jerry blinked. "I'd consider cutting the old-and-tired part."

Melissa shrugged. "I'll think about it."

A figure materialized in Jerry's peripheral vision. He turned to see Zoey standing at the edge of the yard. She wore sunglasses and a leather jacket. She was certainly dressing her image, Jerry thought. He'd never seen her looking so cool.

He waved at her. "Hey, Zoey," he called. "Melissa, you can start going through the first scene. We'll practice here, under the tree. I'll be right back."

Jerry strode across the yard.

Zoey stood at the edge of his mother's garden, her hands stuffed into her jeans pockets.

"Hey, Zoey," Jerry said. "What's up?"

"Problem," she said.

"What problem?"

"Elena doesn't believe two guys are interested in her," Zoey said. "Thinks it's a plot."

"A plot?"

"To mess with her mind."

"Wow," Jerry said. "I guess nobody's been interested in Elena before this, and now, all of a sudden, two guys are . . . well, they're—"

"Hot for her."

"Yeah." Jerry looked away and back at Zoey. "Do you think Cinnamon knows about Sandy?"

"She's beginning to figure it out."

"And Elena thinks it's all a trick?"

Zoey nodded.

"It never occurred to me that this would be a problem," Jerry said. "Elena has less self-esteem than I thought." He shook his head. "Dorkdom runs deep."

"Jer-ry!" Melissa called from under the tree. "Hurry up! We need you."

"I'll be right there," Jerry said. To Zoey, he asked, "You can't convince her these guys are truly interested?"

"Not yet."

Melissa tromped over to Jerry and Zoey. "Come *now*," she said. She stopped and gazed up at Zoey. "Who's that?"

"This is Zoey Long," Jerry said. "She's new in town from Hollywood. Zoey, this is my sister, Melissa."

"You're really from Hollywood?" Melissa asked, her voice rising an octave in her excitement. "Hey, you wanna come and see our play? I bet you could help a *lot*."

"Oh, Melissa," Jerry said. "I don't think Zoey—"

"What's the play?" Zoey asked.

"It's called *Camouflage Girl.*" She said it with pride. "It's really a cool play."

Zoey smiled slightly. "Okay." She started off for the tree and the first graders.

Melissa's face opened into a surprised smile. "Wow!" she said and ran off after Zoey.

Jerry followed.

"Let me tell you the story," Melissa said, skipping sideways. They reached the tree. "See, there's this fairy—it's me, but I'm just *pretending* that I'm this fairy named Snowflake—and I come to school on the first day pretending to be a real girl, and the kids believe me for a while, but pretty soon this other girl comes up and says she doesn't believe I'm really human, and—"

"You're pretending to be human?" Zoey asked.

"Yeah!" Melissa said. "My character is. She's

researched the whole thing, and—"

"You'll need a very cool hairstyle," Zoey told her.

Jerry stood under the tree, watching.

"Like what?" Melissa asked, her eyes widening.

Jerry watched. He could see his reflection in Zoey's sunglasses, looking smaller than he really was and somewhat distorted.

"I'll show you after the rehearsal."

"*Really?*" Melissa cried. "Great!" She looked at Jerry and beamed. "This is so cool! It's going to be the best play in the whole world!"

Jerry nodded and smiled. But he couldn't help wondering why Zoey would spend time on Melissa. He wondered if Zoey was developing her magical powers to manipulate people in other ways, beyond getting them to notice Elena.

Oh, well, he thought. Maybe Zoey can really help. After all, what did he know about directing a play?

He smiled and said, "Okay, let's get to work."

"I *love* this hairstyle!" Melissa danced around the living room. "I look *wonderful!*"

Jerry stared at her and wondered what in the world their parents would say.

Zoey had given his little sister a new style, all right. Her hair was heavily greased with mousse and stood up in about twenty-five little spikes all over her head.

What was she *thinking?*

"Do I look cool, or what?" Melissa admired herself in the living room mirror that hung over the couch.

Zoey stood off to the side, her arms folded over her chest, smiling slightly. Her sunglasses were still in place, even though the sun was beginning to sink outside and the natural light in the living room was dimming.

Jerry frowned and mouthed the word "why?" to Zoey, but she didn't respond. Maybe she wasn't looking at him; Jerry couldn't tell.

Jerry shook his head. Zoey's magic could do good things and not so good things.

Besides Elena's misinterpretation of Gabe's and Sandy's attention, Zoey's magic was doing good things for Elena. It was making her popular for maybe the first time in her life.

But Melissa's new hairstyle? Jerry watched his sister twirl and leap in front of the mirror, admiring her hair, which made her look like a greasy porcupine.

This was one of the not so good things.

Chapter Ten

Jerry sat on his bedroom floor, and Melissa sat next to him, scowling, her arms folded across her chest. Jerry held two objects: an empty soda can and a blown-up balloon. The room smelled of the mousse that was still holding Melissa's hair up in small points all over her head.

"I don't see why Mom won't let me wear my hair this way to school," she muttered.

It wasn't a time for tact.

"Because, Melissa, it looks really stupid," he said.

"It does *not*! Zoey thinks it's cool, and she's from Hollywood. No offense, Jerry, but Mom and Dad and you wouldn't know, because you're not cool, like Zoey."

"I think Zoey was teasing you," Jerry said. He placed the soda can on its side on the hardwood floor and touched it with his finger, making sure it didn't roll. "It's the only explanation. Now, come on, I'll show you a science trick."

"I don't want to see it."

"Well, I'm going to show you anyway." Jerry was hoping he could pull Melissa out of her sullen mood. He held the balloon up to his head and rubbed it hard on his hair.

Melissa refused to watch.

"I'm rubbing it on my hair," he told her.

"So?"

He brought the balloon down next to the can, and slowly moved the balloon away. The can started to roll after it.

"Look, Missy," Jerry said. "The can's following the balloon."

Melissa didn't turn her head, but he saw that she watched from the corner of her eye.

"See?" Jerry said. "This is pretty cool."

"How does it work?" Melissa asked, in spite of herself.

"Rubbing the balloon on my hair loaded it with electrons, which are subatomic particles that have a negative charge. Then the electrons on the balloon attracted the protons in the soda can and pulled it along, like a magnet. Isn't it cool?"

Melissa sighed loudly. "What*ever*."

* * *

"Jerry, can I talk to you?"

"Sure, Cinnamon."

The early-morning sunshine beamed through the branches of the oak overhead. Jerry leaned against it, waiting for Brenda. The school grounds were fast filling up with students arriving for school.

Cinnamon stopped in front of Jerry. She wore a fire-engine red sweater that made Jerry's eyes hurt. He wondered if she wanted to be noticed today.

He answered himself in his head. Of course she did! Was there ever a day in Cinnamon's whole life when she *didn't* want to be noticed?

"You know that girl, Elena somebody?" Cinnamon asked.

Oh-oh. He knew what was coming. And he knew why Cinnamon had chosen to wear this particular sweater today.

"Yeah, Elena Charles."

"Well, I get the feeling . . ." Cinnamon glanced over her shoulder, looking uncomfortable. Then she looked over the other shoulder, turned back to Jerry, and lowered her voice to a whisper. "Well, this is just for your ears. But it seems like Sandy's kind of—well, as hard as it is to *believe* . . ."

"Yes?"

"Well, it seems like Sandy's actually—kind of—*interested* in her."

Jerry was curious. "That's hard to believe?"

"Well, yeah," Cinnamon said, frowning. "I mean, she's cool and everything, but . . ."

"Yeah?"

Cinnamon was plainly looking for the right words. "Well, you've seen her, haven't you?"

"Yeah, she's nice."

"Oh. Well. Yeah, she might be nice, but. . ." She made an exasperated noise and the words tumbled out of her mouth in a rush. "Okay, I give up trying to say it nicely. Just think about it, Jerry. Pretend we're standing side by side right here in front of you. *Now* you see what I mean?"

Jerry didn't. He frowned.

"I'm *much* cuter than she is!"

"Ohhh." Jerry didn't know what to say. At least she hadn't said that Elena was a dork. But Cinnamon was expecting him to agree with her about the cute part.

"Well?" Cinnamon said, her eyes wide, staring at him. "Don't you think I'm much cuter than she is? I mean, *really*?"

For a moment, he was speechless. Then he said, "Cinnamon, maybe Sandy doesn't think that looks are the most important thing about a girl."

Cinnamon blinked. "He doesn't?"

"Well, I don't know. But maybe he likes something else about Elena."

Cinnamon frowned again and looked baffled. "Like *what*?"

"Well, as I said, she's nice. And she's smart. And she's—well, she's interesting. Maybe Sandy likes those things."

"Nice, smart, and interesting?" Cinnamon asked, wrinkling her nose. "You think that's what he likes about her?" They seemed to be brand-new concepts to her.

"Could be."

"Nice. Smart. And interesting." Cinnamon whispered the words and considered them for a long moment. She stared at the grass and frowned. Finally, she looked up at him. "No way. That's impossible. Guys don't care about that stuff." She gazed off into the trees. "It must be something else. Do you think she's rich?"

"Not that I know of."

"Maybe her dad drives some fancy-shmancy car, and Sandy wants to get a ride in it."

"I don't know, but I doubt it."

"Well, there's *something* going on that I don't know about." She scowled. "Thanks a lot for all the help, Jerry." She turned and stalked off.

Jerry took a deep breath. He heard soft laughter behind him and turned to see Brenda.

"Sorry," she said. "I couldn't help overhearing."

Jerry shook his head. "You have to admit it: when Cinnamon's around, it's never dull."

"That's true."

"Bren, I'm really sorry about the dog. I thought about it all night."

"It's not your fault," she said. "You did everything you could. And I think you're right; Craig probably planned on keeping her all along."

Robin appeared out of the milling crowd.

"So, Jerry. You going to give the speech at the festival wearing a dress?"

Jerry had to nip this in the bud. He didn't want anyone starting rumors that he might actually go through with it. So he said firmly, "No, I'm not, Robin."

Robin frowned. "You won't even consider it? *Come on!* You'd eat dog food in front of the whole class, but you won't wear a dress for a few minutes?"

"That's right."

"Too bad," Robin said. "That would've been really funny."

Jerry was irritated that she'd think so little of his feelings. "To you, maybe."

"Well, let's face it, Jerry," she said. "You've been humiliated *dozens* of times at school. It seems that wearing a dress wouldn't be too much worse than the other stuff. And it would be so totally hilarious for the rest of us."

Jerry felt as if he'd been hit right between the eyes. He stared hard at Robin and said the words firmly: "You'll have to get your entertainment somewhere else."

"Okay for you," Robin said, her face sullen. "Some sixth-grade president you are. Don't you know you're supposed to bow to the wishes of your voters?"

Jerry was surprised. "Did you vote for me, Robin?"

"Well, no, but—"

"Bye, Robin."

Robin made a face and disappeared into the crowd.

Brenda gazed at Jerry and touched his arm. "Sorry," she said. "I can see that hurt you."

"I guess I don't want to talk about it, Bren," Jerry said, turning away. "I'm tired of being everybody's source of amusement."

Craig was already at the locker when Jerry arrived. Jerry was still stinging from Robin's comment that one more embarrassment on top of the mountains of humiliation he'd already suffered since school started wouldn't make any difference. As if he had no feelings. As if the entire sixth grade got their kicks out of watching him being tormented. Jerry set his jaw. He wasn't in a mood to take any garbage from Craig.

"Hey, Jer," Craig said with a smirk.

"Forget it, Craig," Jerry said. "No."

Craig held out his hands, plastering a what-did-

I-say look on his face. "No what?"

"No, you can't borrow money. No, you can't make me eat more dog food. And, no, I'm not wearing a dress to the festival. Not for you, not for its entertainment value for the sixth grade, not for any reason."

"Whoa. Okay," Craig said. He shrugged. "Well, that means I get to keep the pooch, then."

"I guess it does." Jerry slapped his science book on the shelf and pulled out his language arts and social studies notebooks. He stopped and looked Craig full in the face. "You can keep her."

Craig's face registered profound disappointment that created in Jerry's chest a small bubble of pleasure.

Good, Jerry thought. If he's going to keep the pup locked up in a shed all day, he shouldn't get pleasure out of keeping her from someone who'll really take care of her.

"Okay, let's continue," Ms. Robertson said, holding her copy of *A Midsummer Night's Dream*. "So what's going on with Bottom, our silly actor, in this scene?"

Brenda spoke up. "Puck uses his magic to give Bottom the head of a donkey."

"It's really the head of an ass," Cinnamon piped up.

Brenda turned in her seat. "I just wanted you to

understand what I meant," she said.

"Like I wouldn't?" asked Cinnamon. "I know what an ass is." She slapped a hand over her mouth and turned red.

Snorts of laughter filled the room.

"Okay, everyone," Ms. R. said, smiling. "Now that we've established which *kind* of ass we're talking about, let's go on with our discussion."

Jerry smiled. He had a mental picture of Bottom with his donkey head, marching around the woods. Puck's magic could do some pretty funny things.

He blinked, a new image coming to mind. It came from Zoey's magic. A six-year-old prancing around the living room, wearing that ridiculous hairstyle that Zoey had given her.

Jerry turned back to look at the coolest girl in the sixth grade.

Zoey sat in her seat in the back of the room. Her head was tipped down to look at the book on her desk. But her eyes rose to meet Jerry's.

And she grinned just a little.

Chapter Eleven

Later that morning, Jerry met Brenda at her locker, and they headed to their math class. As they reached the top of the stairs, they looked down the main corridor and saw a gathering of students. Loud voices sounded above the rest of the normal clamor.

"What's going on?" Jerry asked.

"I don't know. Let's go see."

As they got nearer, he heard Cinnamon's voice rise above the rest. "Sandy, I just don't understand!"

Jerry and Brenda arrived at the clump of students. Gabe and Sandy and Elena and Cinnamon faced off, each looking angry and confused. A crowd of students had gathered to watch.

"Why are you always hanging around Elena?" Cinnamon cried.

"Oh, stop it, Cinnamon," Elena said. "I'm so tired of this little joke. It's gone way too far."

"What are you *talking* about?" Cinnamon demanded. "What little joke? I just want to know why Sandy's paying so much attention to you."

"Because, Cinnamon," Sandy said, "this is a free country, and I like Elena. So stop bugging me, okay?"

Cinnamon's mouth dropped open. "Stop bugging you? I thought we were going out!"

"Not anymore." Sandy gazed at Elena with longing in his eyes. "I swear, Elena. Not anymore."

"Elena," Gabe said, "I don't know what's going on with these two maniacs, but I've been trying to—"

"You!" Elena cried. "Gabe, you're the worst of all! You've been a jerk to me since school started, and now you're pretending to like me!"

"I'm not pretending to like you!" Gabe said. "Why would I do that?"

Cinnamon stepped in front of Elena and pushed her face to within six inches of the tall girl's chin. "You stole Sandy from me! And you're not even cute! You're like this *giant*—this telephone-pole girl. You're a tree person, walking around the halls, talking to all the boys who are all up there at your height."

"What?" Elena cried. "You're holding that against

me? Just because you're short—"

"I'm not *short*! Unlike you, I'm cute and *normal*!" Cinnamon whirled on Sandy. "Is *that* what you like about her? Her *height*? Give me a break! I could understand if she's rich or beautiful or something. But *tall*?"

"Tall has nothing to do with it," Sandy said, rolling his eyes.

"Then how did she *do* it?" Cinnamon demanded. "What does she have that I don't have?"

"You name it," both Sandy and Gabe said at the same time.

Cinnamon shrieked and flew at Elena, who scrambled backward until she hit a locker.

Jerry and Brenda grabbed Cinnamon's arms. "Okay," Jerry said. "That's enough."

"You're ridiculous," Brenda said. "All of you. Cinnamon, what's the matter with you? You can't just attack someone because you're angry."

Ms. Robertson appeared and pushed through the crowd. "What's going on here?" she demanded.

"It's over, Ms. R.," Jerry said.

"It's time for you all to get to your classes," Ms. R. said in a loud voice. *"Now."*

Cinnamon huffed loudly and headed off down the hall. Elena, whose face was beet red, hurried away. Sandy turned in the opposite direction, and Gabe trudged off, following Cinnamon.

The small crowd dwindled as students left for

their classes. Ms. R. stood watching Jerry, who nodded to her. He turned Brenda around and walked her down the hall toward math class.

"Flack."

It was just before lunch when Jerry heard his name called out in a low voice. He was late getting to the cafeteria because he'd had to stop at his locker to get his science book.

He turned to see Gabe standing at the intersection of two halls. "Come here." Gabe jerked his head to one side, beckoning him to follow him around the corner.

Jerry felt his body stiffen. He didn't trust Gabe. Almost every time Jerry had come near Gabe in the past, Gabe had done something underhanded that had either humiliated him or made him angry.

Jerry didn't move. He took a slow, calming breath. "What do you want?"

Gabe's face registered understanding. "Oh, come on, Flack, it's okay. I'm not going to try anything. I just want to talk to you. Honest."

Jerry studied Gabe's face. He wasn't wearing his usual smirk, and he had a sad look in his eyes.

Could he actually trust Gabe? Was this time any different?

"Why don't you come here?" Jerry suggested. He gazed off down the hall, one way and then the other. "Nobody's around. They all went to lunch."

Gabe rolled his eyes, but shuffled over to Jerry, who kept a safe distance from the lockers, in case Gabe decided to give him a shove.

"I just wanted to ask you about that committee you're on."

Jerry frowned. "The committee?"

"Yeah," Gabe said. "You asked me if I wanted to be on it."

"The sixth-grade committee?" Jerry asked. "You said you weren't interested."

"Well, I changed my mind."

"You did?"

"Yeah."

Jerry couldn't believe it. "You want to be on the committee to think of cool things for the sixth grade?"

"That's what I said, isn't it?"

"How come?" Jerry blurted. He really wanted to know.

"Why shouldn't I?" Gabe asked. There was no mistaking the edge in his voice.

Then Jerry realized the reason.

"Oh. Because Elena's on it, right?"

"No way," Gabe said quickly. But his face betrayed him, turning a deep red.

Jerry didn't want Gabe on the committee. The people serving on it were very cool, and Gabe's presence would undoubtedly make it less fun. But off the top of his head, he couldn't think of a good reason to give Gabe for keeping him off.

"Well," Jerry said slowly, "I guess you could be on it if you want to."

"When's the next meeting?"

"Next week. Monday, fifth period."

Jerry saw Gabe's whole body relax. "Good," he said.

"In Mr. Hooten's room," Jerry added.

"Okay." Gabe started to turn away, but turned back. "Uh. Thanks."

Jerry felt his eyebrows rise. It was a novel experience, hearing Gabe express appreciation. "No problem."

Jerry watched Gabe saunter away down the hall. Now, *that*, he thought, was an interesting meeting.

Craig and Gabe walked with their lunch trays across the cafeteria.

"Hey, Flack," Craig said, pausing at Jerry's table. "Just a reminder that you can get the dog next Friday if you really want it." He grinned at Gabe. "Right, Marshall?"

Gabe glanced back at Craig but continued across the cafeteria.

"Looks like you're alone this time, Craig," Brenda said, her eyes narrowing with anger. "Gabe isn't impressed, and neither are we."

"Don't you want the little doggy, Flack?" Craig asked with a smirk.

"Not that way." Jerry didn't even look up at him.

"Well, there's no other way," Craig said. "Take it or leave it."

Jerry turned to face his tormentor and said simply, "I'll leave it, Craig."

Craig's smirk faded. "Okay, Flack." He shrugged and took a step backward. "But if you change your mind, you know where to find me."

"We're locker partners, Craig," Jerry said flatly. "I wouldn't have much trouble finding you. But I won't change my mind."

Craig shrugged as if he didn't care and strode off.

No one at Jerry's table spoke for a moment. He knew they were all looking at him, waiting for him to say something.

He also knew that Craig was just tormenting him to impress Gabe and to embarrass him in front of his friends. He'd made it clear this morning that he had no intention of wearing a dress to the Elizabethan Festival.

He picked up his grilled cheese sandwich and took a bite, staring at the off-white surface of the table. He chewed the bread and cheese mechanically, not tasting them, not exactly aware that they were in his mouth.

"Jerry?" It was Kat.

Jerry looked up.

"Are you sure you don't want to consider wearing a dress during the speech?"

Jerry gawked at her and lowered the sandwich in his hand. *"What?"*

"I mean, it's the life of a helpless creature."

"I always thought you were crazy," Kim said to her sister, shaking her head. "And this proves it."

Kat ignored the remark. "Balanced against the life of a little dog, what does it matter if you're embarrassed for a while?"

Jerry felt heat pulsing in his body. He couldn't believe that Kat thought he should wear a dress during his speech.

"Easy for you to say." He felt the anger growing inside him.

"Kat, that's not fair," Brenda said. "Nobody can ask Jerry to humiliate himself on purpose. He's been through enough this year already."

Jerry sat up, ready to defend himself. "Besides, you think that would be the end of it? You think I could embarrass my parents and not get grounded? Or let down Ms. Robertson, who's been so nice to me? Or be taunted about it for the rest of my natural life? Or have the presidency taken away from me? After all I went through to win the election? I'd have to hide my face every day at school! Everyone would know what I did, how I'd degraded myself. I'd have to *move out of town.*"

Kat nodded. "I know what you're saying, and I understand." She sighed. "But the puppy . . ."

"You can't do it, Jerry," Tony murmured. "Not

even for the little dog."

"Not even for the puppy," Brenda agreed.

But Jerry heard the sadness in her voice.

He wanted to scream and slug Craig because he was so frustrated and angry. He wanted to demand that Craig give Brenda the pup.

But he knew he wouldn't do any of that. Jerry wasn't that kind of guy. And, besides, it wouldn't work. Punching out Craig would only make him more determined than ever to keep the dog so Brenda and he couldn't have her.

Jerry was stuck between a rock and a very hard place. He couldn't move in any direction and get satisfaction. And save the pup. And make Brenda happy.

Not without humiliating himself in the process.

And he just couldn't do that.

Chapter Twelve

"Not a lot of games from the late sixteenth century are known," Mr. Gunther said. "So we're going to play a game that's from the late seventeenth century, but it's probably pretty similar to games played a hundred years earlier during Elizabethan times."

Jerry and Brenda stood beside the athletic field behind the building after school. Jerry counted twenty sixth graders who had come to the Friday after-school class on Elizabethan games that their PE teacher was leading.

Brenda had persuaded him to come. He knew Brenda was only trying to cheer him up, and he didn't have the heart to tell her that he wasn't in the mood to play games, that he usually *hated* games, unless it was on a board or computer.

He looked up to see Elena come out of the school and walk over to the field. He tilted his head at Brenda, signaling her to follow, then edged over to Elena.

"I thought you were taking the stage combat class," he murmured to her.

"Yeah, but Gabe's there," she said in a low voice. "So I thought I'd try something else today."

Mr. Gunther raised his voice. "Okay, let's walk out to the middle of the field. We're going to play barleybreak. It's an easy game played in pairs, similar to tag."

Jerry, Elena, and Brenda walked with the rest of the students out onto the field.

"Gabe really does like you, you know," Jerry said to Elena.

She frowned. "You mean, you believe him, too? Even Zoey believes him."

"Sure," Jerry said. "In fact, this morning, he asked to be on our sixth-grade committee just because *you're* on it."

Elena held out a hand to stop him; she stared hard into his face. "Are you *serious*? You're not making that up?"

Jerry shrugged. "Why would I make up a thing like that?"

Elena seemed to be weighing Jerry's evidence.

She frowned. "Did he *tell* you he wanted to be on the committee because of me?"

"Well, no, but when I asked him if that was the reason, he got bright red."

"Really? Gabe *blushed?*"

"Fire-engine red."

She pursed her lips thoughtfully.

"What?" Jerry asked.

"I'm having trouble picturing Gabe feeling embarrassed."

"I know what you mean," Jerry said, "but I saw it with my own eyes. And you'll get proof Monday that he meant it. He'll be at the meeting in Mr. Hooten's room."

"It's true, Elena," Brenda added. "Gabe's not faking you out. Really."

Elena continued to mull it over. "Gee, it's so hard to believe."

"Why?" Jerry asked her. "You're a cool person. Zoey recognizes that, and now everybody else is seeing it, too." He looked up to see that the students were all ahead of them. "Come on."

They trudged toward the center of the field.

"Hey, Elena!"

Jerry, Brenda, and Elena looked over to see Sandy Powers walking toward them. Just behind him, waving her arms, ran Cinnamon.

"Sandy!" she hollered. "Where're you going?"

He turned to her. "What do you want?"

"I just wondered where you're going."

Sandy gestured to the group of sixth graders.

"Sorry, but seventh graders aren't allowed," Cinnamon said. "It's only for sixth because we're studying *A Midsummer Night's Dream.*" Her head turned, and she saw Elena. "No, you definitely *can't* stay. Gunther will throw you off the field."

Sandy ignored her and joined the sixth graders.

"But, Sandy . . ."

Jerry watched as Sandy positioned himself so he could see Elena. Cinnamon stared at him, her eyes narrowed.

Jerry looked at Brenda and lifted his eyebrows. A figure in the distance over Brenda's shoulder drew his attention. It was Gabe, walking in their direction.

"Oh-oh," Jerry murmured. He hoped there wouldn't be a repeat of the sparks that had flown this morning in the hall.

Elena turned to see Gabe.

"You see that?" Jerry asked her. "You think he's coming out here because he wants to play an Elizabethan tag game?"

Jerry saw a new light come into Elena's eyes, and he knew that she finally realized Gabe actually *did* like her.

"He must've followed me out here." She drew in a breath and a look of horror passed over her face.

"What's wrong?" Jerry asked. "Aren't you happy?

You said you've always had a crush on him."

"But I've been *horrible* to him." Elena put her hands to her face. "I even *yelled* at him."

Gabe approached the edge of the group slowly. He looked shy.

Jerry was astounded. He thought that nothing else, for the rest of his life, would surprise him. Now he'd seen everything: Gabe had looked both shy and embarrassed in the same day.

"Okay, everyone," Mr. Gunther called out. "Choose partners. We'll break into groups of three pairs."

A buzz rose from the students on the field as they chose partners.

"Well, okay, Sandy, I guess you can stay here with us sixth graders," Cinnamon announced. "We'll be partners." She grabbed his hand. "Come on, let's go over there." She pointed away from Elena and pulled at his hand.

"Let *go*." Sandy yanked his hand free.

Cinnamon's eyebrows crept together and her lower lip slid out, but she kept quiet.

Brenda took Jerry's hand, and they watched as the other students finished pairing up.

Elena looked at Jerry with a quizzical expression.

Jerry grinned at her. "Yup," he said. "This will be interesting to watch."

"The burning question," Brenda murmured, "is what will Gabe do now?"

"I think I'll help him," Elena said. "You *sure* he likes me?"

"Positive."

"Okay," she said. "I can't believe I'm doing this, but I've played hard to get long enough."

She walked over to Gabe and spoke softly to him.

A look of profound relief passed over his face. He smiled and nodded. Brenda grinned at Jerry and squeezed his hand.

Mr. Gunther separated the students into groups of three pairs. Jerry and Brenda were in a group with Elena and Gabe. Jerry tried to maneuver them all away from Cinnamon and Sandy, but Mr. Gunther indicated with big gestures who would be in each group, and he put them all together.

Sandy allowed Cinnamon to continue holding his hand, but his eyes hung on Elena, who stood next to Gabe.

"Okay," Mr. Gunther called out, "in a minute, one pair in your group will go to the end of the field. Another pair will go to the opposite end. The remaining pair stays here in the middle. We start the game with partners holding hands. The first pair at the north end will start by shouting, 'Barley!' and the pair at the south end will answer, 'Break!'

"At that time, everyone drops hands. The four players at the ends of the field start running toward each other and their new partners at the other end of the field. Get that? The girl at the north end and the boy at the south end will run toward each other. And the boy at the north end and the girl at the south end will run toward each other.

"If either of the two people in the middle catches anyone before that person meets his or her new partner, that new couple has to go to the center of the field, and the people in the center go to either end. If two people are caught, the first person caught must go to the center with his or her new partner. If the pairs on the end reach their new partners before they're caught, the pair in the middle stays there. Then the new pairs go to either ends of the field for the next round." He looked around. "Any questions?"

"I think I followed that," Jerry murmured.

"We'll be on the north end," Sandy volunteered. "Jerry, you and Brenda can be in the middle."

"Why?" Cinnamon asked. Her eyes took on the look of understanding. "Ohhh, I get it." She glared at Elena. "It's *her* again! You want to run to her and become her partner. I *hate* this game!"

"But we'll play several rounds, Cinnamon," Brenda said. "Our pairs will get mixed up with each round. You'll be back soon with Sandy."

Cinnamon dropped Sandy's hand and strode over to Elena. She leaned in, but Jerry heard her say, "If you know what's good for you, girl, you won't stay partners with Sandy very long."

"Cinnamon," Elena said, "I want to be Gabe's partner."

Cinnamon whirled around to face Sandy. "You hear that? The telephone pole says she wants to be *Gabe's* partner. So forget her; it's hopeless for you."

"Hey, Cinnamon," called out Gabe. "Cut out the name-calling, or I'm going to start calling you 'shrimp.'"

"I'm not a shrimp!" Cinnamon shouted.

"Come on," Jerry said. "Let's just play, okay? Mr. Gunther's ready to start."

Cinnamon marched back to Elena. "And you're supposed to be holding hands," she said. She grabbed Gabe's and Elena's hands and smacked them together. "There. Now *stay* that way as long as possible." Gabe grinned at Elena, while Cinnamon returned to Sandy's side and grabbed his hand again.

"Okay," called out Mr. Gunther. "Everyone go to your starting place. One pair at the north end of the field, one at the south, one in the middle."

Jerry and Brenda trudged to the center of the field.

"An interesting turn of events," Brenda said. "I'm glad you were able to convince Elena that Gabe likes her."

"Me, too," Jerry answered. "That's half the battle, I guess."

"Right. Now if Sandy would only start liking Cinnamon again."

"She's trying too hard," Jerry said.

"Yeah, I'd go that far."

When all couples were in their places, Mr. Gunther nodded. "Let's start," he shouted.

Elena and Gabe dropped hands and yelled, "Barley!"

Sandy shook off Cinnamon's clutching hand and shouted, "Break!"

They started running. Jerry expected that Sandy would break all land speed records to run to Elena, so he could be her partner.

Jerry started running north, hoping to tag either Sandy or Cinnamon, while Brenda headed south.

Jerry watched Sandy as he hurled himself down the field toward Elena. Coming close, the seventh grader stretched out his arms to catch her. But something unexpected happened.

Instead of heading toward Gabe, her new partner, Cinnamon chose instead to run after Sandy. When he was a couple of feet from Elena, Cinnamon grabbed his outstretched arm, and with an amazing amount of strength, yanked him away from her. Sandy jerked toward Cinnamon, and at that precise moment, with surprising grace, she extended her right foot and tripped him.

Jerry watched poor Sandy stumble to the ground and roll twice before coming to a stop, face-down in the grass.

Jerry stopped running and slowly approached the fallen boy.

"Sandy, are you all right?" he asked.

Cinnamon fell to her knees at his side. "Are you okay, Sandy? I'm so sorry, I accidentally tripped you!"

Sandy rolled over and scowled at Cinnamon. "Riiight."

"What?" Cinnamon cried, her voice high. "You don't believe me? It was an accident! I swear!"

"So what do we do now?" Elena asked. "Mr. Gunther didn't say what to do if somebody trips her own partner."

"I didn't trip him!" hollered Cinnamon. "Is it my fault he's a doofus? He's clumsy and tripped over his own feet."

"Thanks, Cinnamon," Sandy said, glancing self-consciously at Elena.

"I guess Brenda and I will be in the middle again," Jerry said. "This time, Cinnamon, head toward Gabe, your new partner. Brenda and I will try to catch somebody again."

"But I don't want to be partners with Gabe!" Cinnamon cried. "Elena deserves to be with him. See? I'm trying to be *nice* to her."

"This game is deteriorating fast," Brenda murmured.

"It's a stupid game anyway," said Cinnamon.

Jerry held up his hand. "Maybe we should just agree that this game isn't working and go home."

"I think we should play a couple of rounds," Sandy said, still gazing with longing at Elena.

"Hey, leave her alone," Gabe growled at Sandy.

Sandy took a step toward him. "Want to make me?"

"With pleasure."

Gabe started toward Sandy, but Elena planted herself between the two boys. "Okay, you guys. Stop it."

"Oh." Gabe stopped suddenly, as if he'd just realized that Elena probably wouldn't like it if he threw a punch. "Okay." He put an arm around her. "Come on, I'll walk you home."

The two of them strolled off. Sandy stood there, blinking sad eyes, watching them go.

Jerry couldn't help feeling a little sorry for him. He'd tried very hard to get Elena's attention, and he was obviously hurting because he'd lost the battle for Elena with Gabe.

"I'm going home!" Cinnamon announced. "That is, if anybody cares."

Sandy obviously didn't care. He didn't even glance at her. He started off, trudging across the field.

That left Jerry standing between Cinnamon and Brenda. Both were quiet.

Jerry shifted his weight and stared at the ground. He cleared his throat. "Well."

"Thanks for the great game, Jerry," Cinnamon said sarcastically. She turned and stormed off in the opposite direction.

"'Thanks for the great game, Jerry'?" he said. "It wasn't even my game."

Brenda sighed. "Come on. Let's go home. It's been a long day."

But it wasn't my game, Jerry repeated silently. I don't even *like* games.

Chapter Thirteen

$\int$ erry and Brenda sat under the maple in Jerry's backyard. Items for a science experiment were strewn on the grass in front of them. It was Saturday, and Jerry usually loved Saturdays. It was supposed to be a day of relaxation and fun, two days away from the next school day.

But today Jerry was feeling bad. He stared at the box of baking soda in front of him, not really seeing it. He wasn't even in the mood for science experiments.

"Everything that's going on in my life right now is so messed up," Jerry said. "And I'm responsible for all of it." He ticked off the various situations on his fingers. "The little dog is still cooped up—probably hungry—in Craig's shed; I'm trying to get Melissa and her friends prepared to do their play, and they're not ready; I have to give a speech next Friday at the festival, and I haven't started thinking about what I'm going to say; and by asking Zoey to help make Elena more popular, I've made Sandy and Cinnamon miserable. I never should have interfered in their lives."

"Okay," Brenda said. "First of all, you've tried hard to get the puppy away from Craig; you ate *dog food* to rescue her, for pete's sake. You still have time to get Melissa's play ready. They *are* performing it Thursday, right? Same with the speech: you have plenty of time to write what you're going to say. And you were just trying to help Elena; your motives were beyond reproach."

"Thanks, Brenda," Jerry said. "But having sincere motives isn't good enough, if I make people—or a little dog—unhappy. And Gabe probably would've noticed Elena eventually, anyway. She really is a cool person."

"Come on," Brenda said. "Show me the science trick you promised. Then we'll talk about your speech, and you'll have one less thing to feel bad about."

Jerry sighed. "Okay." He looked at the stuff spread out on the grass. "This is a bubbly bomb."

"Did you say a bomb?"

"Yeah. But it's made out of fizzy bubbles."

Jerry took a paper towel and tore off a five-inch square. Then he picked up the baking soda and measured one and a half tablespoons. He put the soda in the middle of the piece of paper towel. He folded the paper into thirds and then into thirds again, making a packet around the soda.

"Okay, now, the liquids," he said and picked up a plastic bag with a zip top. "I tested it to make sure it doesn't have holes in it. That's important."

Into the plastic bag he poured a half cup of vinegar from a bottle and a quarter cup of warm water from a glass at his knee.

"This is the part that can be kind of hard," he said. "I'm going to drop the paper towel with the soda into the water and get it closed as fast as possible."

"Why don't you zip it about halfway closed, then slip in the paper towel?" Brenda suggested.

"Brilliant," Jerry said. "See why I like having you around?"

Brenda tilted her head and smiled. "Is that the *only* reason?"

It was the closest Brenda had ever come to flirting with him. Jerry grinned. "I could think of a few others." He had a strong urge to kiss her, but he suddenly wondered if his mother might be gazing out the window of her office upstairs, so he decided to wait for a more private opportunity.

He closed the bag halfway, slid the paper towel

packet inside, and quickly zipped the bag so it was tightly closed.

"Now I'll shake it a little. And stand back!"

He set the bag on the ground, and he and Brenda scrambled back out of the way.

The bag suddenly puffed out, straining its sides.

BANG! The plastic bag exploded with a loud noise, and fizzy bubbles splashed onto the grass all around it.

"Cool!" Brenda said. "That was a good one. It has the same scientific principles as the volcano you made a few weeks ago, right?"

"Right," Jerry said. "When we combine vinegar and baking soda, carbon dioxide is produced, which fills the plastic bag and finally bursts it open."

"Melissa would've liked that one."

"I'll show her later."

"Is she still wearing her hair in little spikes?" Brenda asked.

"Every chance she gets."

"And no one's ever told her she looks strange that way?"

"Oh, we tell her that all the time," Jerry said. "But because Zoey led her to believe it was cool, we can't convince her."

Brenda gazed at Jerry thoughtfully. "What do you think it is about Zoey that makes everyone follow her?"

"I've been thinking about that," Jerry said. "It's amazing. She's just very cool. And she seems to have a kind of authority. So when she talks, people listen."

"I wish I had that effect on people," Brenda said.

"Me, too," Jerry agreed. "Let's face it, Zoey's magic is powerful." He leaned back on his elbows. "Maybe too powerful. I think I need to do something about Cinnamon and Sandy."

"Like what?"

"Well, they're both unhappy. But they liked each other before Zoey worked her magic on Elena. And you have to admit, they're pretty similar."

"You mean, shallow and empty-headed?"

"Well, yeah." Jerry noticed that Brenda didn't smile. She hadn't meant it as a mean joke; she was just being truthful. "I mean, I shouldn't have messed with their social lives in the first place, but I did. So I think I should try to help them be happy again. Maybe if I can ask Zoey to turn her magic on Cinnamon, everything will work out."

Brenda smiled. "That's a great idea."

"I'll call her later." Jerry gazed at Brenda. "But what are we going to do about the pup?"

Brenda's smile faded. "I don't think we can do anything. We can't take her away from Craig, so we won't get her unless he gives her to us."

Jerry closed his eyes; he felt a headache coming on. Brenda was right. Even if he wrote a good speech and gave it without messing up, and he got the first graders ready to present their play, and if Zoey could convince Sandy that Cinnamon is cool—and that was a lot of *ifs*—they'd still have the worst problem of all: the little dog. What would happen to the pup?

An idea suddenly blossomed in Jerry's mind. "Let's call Craig and see if we can play with the pup for a while."

"Really? You think he'd let us see her?"

"I don't know," Jerry said. "But if he does, and if she's not being fed, we could report him to the animal welfare people. I don't want to get him in trouble, but we can't let him mistreat her."

Brenda's eyes lit up. "Let's do it."

"Why don't you call him, Brenda? I think he'd be more likely to say yes to you than to me."

"You might be right," she said. "Let's go."

They traipsed into the kitchen through the back door. Jerry looked up Craig's number in the phone book, picked up the receiver on the wall phone, and dialed.

"Good luck," he whispered and handed the phone to Brenda.

She put it to her ear and waited.

"Hi," she said. "Is Craig there, please?" She paused. "Oh, he is? Well, I was just wondering if I could . . . Could you tell me where he took her? He's in my class, and I'd love to see the puppy." Another pause. "Okay. Yes, I know where it is. Thanks. Bye."

Brenda's face opened into a big smile, and she hung up the phone. "His mom said he took the puppy to Turtle Creek Park."

"You're kidding. He's playing with her? Let's go."

Jerry and Brenda jogged most of the six blocks to the park.

Turtle Creek Park was divided into upper and lower levels. The upper level covered about thirty acres. On that land were hundreds of trees, scattered picnic tables, and two swimming pools. The lower level had two baseball diamonds, a duck pond with a warming house for the ice-skaters in winter, and a footbridge over the meandering Turtle Creek.

Jerry and Brenda slowed at the park's upper-level entrance.

"I don't see him," Jerry said, breathing hard. "Do you?"

"Uh-uh. Let's walk through this level and look on the other side of the swimming pool. If they're not there, then we'll head to the lower level."

"Right."

On the other side of the swimming pool, Jerry said, "He's not here. Let's go down to the duck pond."

Two routes could take them to the lower level. One was down a steep stairway, set into the side of a hill. The other would take them around the hill and enter the lower level the way traffic did.

"The stairs will be faster," Jerry said.

They descended carefully but stopped halfway down the hill to survey the land below.

"I don't see Craig or the dog," Jerry said. "Let's go get a better look."

They made their way down the rest of the stairs and crossed the baseball diamond, walking toward the warming house.

"What's that noise?" Brenda asked.

A strange commotion, barking and honking, grew louder as they approached.

"It sounds like the puppy—and ducks or geese or something," she said.

"Let's go see. It's on the other side of the warming house."

They rounded the stone building.

"Oh, my gosh!" Brenda cried.

Four gray-and-white geese honked and lunged at the puppy who was backed up against a tree, barking frantically. Two of the geese dipped their heads and thrust forward, trying to bite the pup. She danced out of their way, only to get nipped by a goose who'd circled behind her.

"Stop it! Stop it!"

Brenda and Jerry ran to the ducks, waving their arms and stamping their feet. The noise intensified, but the geese turned away and flutter-waddled toward the pond, honking their displeasure over their shoulders.

Brenda scooped up the puppy. "Oh, you poor thing! How many times did they bite you? You aren't bleeding anywhere that I can see."

"I wonder where Craig is?" Jerry said.

"That rotten Craig Fox!"

The puppy reached up and licked Brenda's face, her tail slapping to either side, a metronome on high speed.

It was only then that Jerry caught sight of a foot dangling among the leaves just over his head. He peered up into the branches.

"Craig?"

The boy straddled a branch. "Yeah?"

"You come down out of that tree right *now*!" Brenda hollered at him. "You coward! You jerk! You climbed the tree and left this poor little puppy to battle those mean geese all by herself? I'm so mad at you Craig Fox, I could just punch you in the nose!"

Craig, who had made some moves to come down from the tree, froze when he heard Brenda's threat.

"Come on, Craig," Jerry said softly. "Brenda's not going to hurt you."

"I knew that."

Craig dropped from the tree in front of them.

"What happened?" Jerry asked. "Why were the geese attacking the dog?"

Craig shrugged.

Jerry spotted Craig's pockets, which were bulging.

"What's in your pockets?" Jerry asked.

"Nothin'."

Jerry tapped the pockets with his fingers. "You have rocks in there?"

"Rocks!" Brenda cried. "What were you doing—throwing rocks at the geese? Is that why they came after you?"

Craig looked worried. "No." It was the most ineffective lie Jerry had ever heard.

"So what *did* happen?" Brenda demanded.

Craig's mouth opened, but nothing came out.

"Jerry, she's still very skinny." Brenda's fingers explored the pup's chest and tummy.

Craig scowled. "I'm feedin' her."

"She looks all worn out," Brenda said. "Poor thing. She was scared to death."

"Craig." Jerry spoke carefully, keeping his voice low and unemotional, even though he was as angry at Craig as he'd ever been. "A dog is something you have to take care of. You need to protect her and feed her and give her a comfortable, safe place to live. Do you really want to keep her? Wouldn't you like to give her a good home?"

The words had just left his lips when he realized he'd made a mistake. He didn't mean to imply that Craig's home wasn't good. But he saw the effect the words had on Craig.

"I'm givin' her a good home," he said, the defensiveness on his face changing quickly to anger. "Give me my dog." He yanked her out of Brenda's arms. "And get out of my face. You're not gettin' her."

He took a few steps away, then turned back with a malicious grin.

"Unless, of course, Flack, you wear a dress to that festival thing."

Chapter Fourteen

"Hello?"

"Hey, Zoey. It's me, Jerry." He sat on the floor in his parents' bedroom, the telephone at his ear. Sassy lay at his side and rested her chin on his thigh.

"Hey."

"I have some good news and a request."

"Okay."

"The good news is that Elena now believes that Gabe likes her," Jerry said. "I talked with her; she doesn't believe that Gabe's playing tricks on her anymore."

"Yeah, she called."

"So she and Gabe are pretty happy, I guess. But

now I feel sorry for Cinnamon and Sandy."

Pause. "Okay."

"Sandy's miserable because Elena chose Gabe over him. And Cinnamon's upset because Sandy doesn't seem to like her anymore."

"So your request is?"

Jerry twisted the telephone cord around his finger. "So, I'm not sure what to do. You think it would help if you worked some magic on Cinnamon? Maybe talk to her in front of Sandy?"

A very long pause followed.

"Zoey?"

"No."

"Oh. Why?"

"Hey. I didn't mind giving Elena attention because she's cool."

Jerry waited, but Zoey was silent. "Yeah?" he said finally.

Jerry heard her sigh. "Cinnamon's not too cool, Jerry."

"She's *not*?" Jerry was astounded. He'd always thought that Cinnamon's level of cool was way off the register.

"She doesn't have a cool bone in her body," Zoey informed him. "She's just popular."

Whoa. This was revolutionary. Jerry had always thought that "popular" *meant* "cool."

"This is hard to take in," Jerry admitted. "I guess I missed something in my research on cool."

"Popularity is something you can develop," Zoey told him. "Cool is something you *are*."

"Really?" In the shadier recesses of his mind, a light was beginning to shine on this new concept. "So most anybody can become popular?"

"Given the right training. Or luck."

"Ah."

"Actually," Zoey said, "no one knows for sure if coolness comes from nature or nurture. I think it's probably both."

"That's very interesting." Actually, it was monumental, Jerry thought.

"Mostly," Zoey said, "it's a *knowing*."

"A knowing?"

"That you have the right to be who you are. That you feel comfortable in your skin."

"What about this: can a person be cool but *not* popular?" Jerry asked.

"Sure," Zoey said. "But that happens when everybody else is so totally ignorant, they can't see the cool that's right in front of them."

"Wow."

"And that's just sad," Zoey said. "Cool is always preferable to popular. Remember when Gabe and Craig were playing tricks on you during the campaign?"

As if I could forget, he thought. It had been the most miserable two weeks of his life. "Don't remind me."

"Well, you stood your ground. You didn't try to be somebody you weren't. That was very cool."

Jerry decided not to mention that he'd tried very hard to be somebody he wasn't when school had first started. It had been pretty pathetic the way he'd told lies about himself so everyone would be impressed. Zoey hadn't moved here yet, so she hadn't observed it.

So maybe cool *was* actually learned, Jerry concluded. He'd learned that he didn't want to pretend to be someone he wasn't.

"But what about Elena?" Jerry asked. "Does she have the knowing?"

"Yeah, but she just forgot. She only needed a little reminder."

"Okay. That makes sense."

"Don't feel bad," Zoey said. "The connection between cool and popular is a commonly held myth."

Not only was this a fascinating conversation, Jerry was also impressed that Zoey was talking so much. He never thought he'd hear her utter this many sentences in a row. He guessed it had something to do with discussing a topic on which she was an expert.

His mind went back to the reason for his call. "Well, isn't there something you could do for Cinnamon?" he asked. "I mean find a way to help her with Sandy?"

"I'll think about it."

"I wouldn't want you to do anything that made you uncomfortable."

"I wouldn't *do* anything that made me uncomfortable."

"Oh. Yeah, right."

It made sense, Jerry thought. If a person has the knowing, she would realize she didn't *have* to do anything that made her uncomfortable.

"Unless it's for personal growth," Zoey added. "You can't grow if you don't take an occasional risk."

Talk about a whole new way of looking at stuff. "Well, this has been enlightening," Jerry said.

"Don't mention it."

"See you at school Monday."

"Right."

Cinnamon entered the language arts classroom Monday morning looking like a different person. Her usual bounce was gone; she slumped a little and shambled into the room, her face long and sullen. Jerry couldn't help noticing that her hair was a mess. Instead of the long curls that usually tumbled down her back, her hair looked as if she hadn't touched it since before she'd gone to bed last night. He remembered her telling Sandy that she used a curling iron on it every day. Today it was uncombed and limp, hanging flat against her head.

"Hey, Cinnamon," Jerry said.

"Don't speak to me," she muttered.

"How come?"

She shuffled past his desk toward her seat in the back. She collapsed into it, sighing heavily. Zoey was already at her desk, but she didn't seem to notice the change in Cinnamon. Zoey's eyes were again behind sunglasses. Her legs stretched out in front of her, and her arms were folded over her chest.

"Hey, Cinnamon," Robin called from her seat. She glanced over at Gabe to get his reaction, but he didn't seem to be paying attention. "What's with your hair?"

Cinnamon didn't even look her way. "I didn't feel like fixing it, and I don't want to talk about it."

Robin seemed to be enjoying this.

"So how's Sandy?" she asked. The look on her face made it obvious that she knew this was a sore point.

"How should I know?" Cinnamon said. "Ask the telephone pole."

"And that would be Elena?" Robin asked, grinning. Gabe now looked up. "That got his attention." She laughed loudly.

"What?"

"I just wondered why Cinnamon is such a mess today," Robin said. "So I asked how Sandy is, and she said I should ask Elena, the telephone pole."

Gabe shrugged. "Elena's going out with me now.

She wouldn't know about Sandy."

Robin's eyes widened, and she clapped her hands. "Ooooooh! Interesting news flash."

Ms. Robertson entered the room as the bell rang. After taking attendance and covering some preliminary material, she started the discussion of *A Midsummer Night's Dream.*

"Okay, we're talking about act three now. Who remembers Puck's famous line about the four protagonists? Anyone?"

"Is it *'Lord, what fools these mortals be!'?"* Jerry asked.

"That's right. Puck's having fun with the mischief he's created. I hope you all read the rest of act three over the weekend. What's going on with our four protagonists? Brenda? How are they getting along?"

"Well, Hermia can't understand why Lysander loves Helena now, instead of her. Hermia and Helena get into a fight."

"That's right," Ms. Robertson said. "Let's read a small part of their argument. Carrie, do you want to read Helena's part? And Cinnamon, why don't you read Hermia's response? Their arguments are fun for the people in the audience because they know that this mix-up is all due to the magic flower. Okay, let's start reading on page eighty-seven."

Carrie found the place in her book and started reading.

"Have you no modesty, no maiden shame,
No touch of bashfulness? What, will you tear
Impatient answers from my gentle tongue?
Fie, fie! you counterfeit, you puppet, you!"

Cinnamon scratched her neck, sighed, and read Hermia's response.

"Puppet? Why, so! Ay, that way goes the
game.
Now I perceive that she had made compare
Between our statures; she hath urged her
height,
And with her personage, her tall personage,
Her height, forsooth, she hath prevailed with
him!"

Cinnamon paused. She looked up and frowned, but continued reading.

"And are you grown so high in his esteem
Because I am so dwarfish and so low?"

Robin snorted with laughter at the back of the room. "Typecasting," she whispered loud enough for everyone to hear.

Cinnamon blinked rapidly and lowered her face closer to the book, but she kept reading.

"How low am I, thou painted maypole?
Speak!
How low am I? I am not yet so low
But that my nails can reach unto thine eyes."

Robin laughed loudly.

Cinnamon looked up from her book. "OKAY," she cried. "That's enough. I don't want to read anymore!"

Gabe watched Cinnamon with interest, and Robin's laughter faded into snickers.

Cinnamon got up, flinging her book onto her desk, and stalked out of the room.

Ms. Robertson looked mystified. "Can anyone tell me what just happened?"

"Um," Jerry said. "Can I . . . ?" He pointed toward the door.

"Yes, please," Ms. R. said, her face registering concern.

Jerry got up and hurried out of the room. He found Cinnamon leaning against a locker at the end of the hall. Her back was to him.

"Hey." He approached and gently touched her shoulder.

She didn't respond.

"Ms. R. didn't choose you to read Hermia because she knew about what's been going on."

"Well, it was embarrassing, anyway. I didn't

understand all of it, but it felt like some of it was, like, my life, you know?"

"I know," Jerry said. "I'm sorry about what happened with Sandy."

Cinnamon turned around, tears filling her eyes. "I just don't get it. Why did he start liking Elena instead of me? What's she got that I don't have?"

"It isn't that," Jerry said.

The guilt monster was dancing around inside his head, pointing its finger and whispering, It's all your fault, Jerry Flack. You did this to the poor girl. You messed with their lives, and now she's miserable.

"Then what is it?" Cinnamon asked.

Jerry didn't want to tell Cinnamon about asking Zoey to perform some magic with Elena. He didn't want her to tell Elena that Sandy only liked her because of Zoey's attention.

"Hey."

Jerry turned to see Zoey standing next to him. Her hands were stuffed into her jeans pockets, her sunglasses riding on the top of her head.

"Hey, Cinnamon," Zoey said. "You don't need Sandy."

Cinnamon blinked. "I don't? But, Zoey, he's so *cool.*"

Zoey rolled her eyes. "If you say so."

"You don't think Sandy's fabulous looking?"

"Yes, I think he's fabulous looking."

"But . . . I don't get it."

Zoey blew out a breath, shook her head, stared at the floor and murmured almost under her breath, *"What dorks these mortals be."* She looked back up at Cinnamon. "Okay. Come here."

She turned Cinnamon around, flung an arm around her shoulder, and they headed off down the hall, Zoey talking softly in Cinnamon's ear.

Jerry watched them go. He didn't know what Zoey was doing, but he figured it might have better results than his feeble attempts to make Cinnamon feel better.

He shrugged and headed back to class.

Chapter Fifteen

Jerry and Brenda stopped at the back of the cafe-teria line. Kim and Kat Henley had already arrived for lunch.

"Hey, guys," Brenda said.

"Hey," they answered in unison.

"Which Elizabethan classes did you guys end up going to?" Brenda asked the sisters.

"I'm in the madrigal singing group," Kat said. "We're fantabulous."

"She says modestly," added Kim.

"Well, we are. You'll be overwhelmed when you hear us Friday night at the festival. I wouldn't be surprised if we're the hit of the evening."

Kim rolled her eyes. "I'm helping to make Elizabethan clothes. You guys will have to come in to get fitted for costumes."

Jerry's stomach clenched. "I still haven't written my speech yet. I sit down to write it, but I don't know what to say other than, 'Welcome. We've been reading *A Midsummer Night's Dream.*' That's not too exciting."

"You're right," Kat said. "So you're not wearing a dress? That would make your speech exciting."

"Of *course* he's not wearing a dress!" Kim and Brenda exploded at the same time.

Kim added, "Dummy."

"Just checking," Kat said.

Kim gazed at the cafeteria entrance. "Hey, look who just walked in."

Kat turned to look. "Elena and Gabe? Wow. When did that happen?"

"After school Friday," Brenda told her.

"What an odd couple," Kat said. "I can't picture them together. She's so smart and nice. And he's so . . . so—"

"Stupid and mean?" Kim asked.

"Yeah."

"I don't think Gabe's stupid," Jerry said. "I think he just likes to act that way."

Kat looked startled. "You mean he acts like an idiot on *purpose*?"

"Yes, right."

Kat looked horrified. "Why on earth would anyone do that?"

Kim rolled her eyes. "Because, dummy, he thinks that idiots are cool."

Kat frowned. "Wait. Let me get this straight. Gabe isn't stupid, but he acts stupid because he thinks it's *cool* to be an idiot?"

"Well, maybe he thinks it's cool to act as if he doesn't care about stuff like school or learning," Jerry said.

Kat sighed. "Boy. Here I am, immersed in sixth grade, but there are so many things about middle-school psychology that I just don't get."

"Don't worry about it, Kat," Jerry said. "I don't always get it, either."

By now, they had worked their way up to the cashier. They paid for their lunches, picked up their food, and started toward their table.

"Hey, Flack," Craig said, walking past alongside Gabe. He reached out and whacked the underside of Jerry's tray. The tray flew out of Jerry's hands, flipped over, and clattered loudly onto the tile floor in front him. Chicken nuggets, plates, and utensils scattered alongside splatters of milk and apple sauce, shreds of lettuce, and glops of chocolate pudding.

Craig hooted and clapped his hands. "That was so cool!"

"Look what you did!" shouted a girl in Jerry's computer class who was now covered with pudding. "These are my best pants, Jerry Flack!"

"Not anymore!" Craig chortled.

"Sorry," Jerry said. *It wasn't my fault,* he wanted to say.

"It wasn't his fault, Stacy," Brenda said. "Craig knocked the tray out of his hands."

Stacy hurried away, muttering to herself.

"Craig's so mean," Kim said.

"Did you see that, Marshall?" Craig called out, still laughing. Gabe had turned back to see what the commotion was about.

"Yeah, I saw it." He scowled at Craig. He stooped to pick up a handful of chicken nuggets, then picked up the fallen tray and tossed the nuggets on top. He handed the tray back to Jerry and muttered, "He's such a nitwit." He turned and walked toward the end of the cafeteria line, followed by Craig.

Jerry stood frozen with the tray in his hand.

"Did you see *that?*" he whispered to Brenda, who had gathered up some pieces of lettuce and put them on the tray.

"Will wonders never cease."

"It's amazing," Jerry said.

Gabe Marshall had actually done something *thoughtful.*

Maybe Zoey wasn't the only person at school

who could influence the behavior of others; maybe Elena had some of those magical powers, too.

"Okay," Jerry said, looking around the table at his sixth-grade committee. "Now let's talk about the festival. How are we doing? Are all the groups ready to demonstrate a part of Elizabethan life?"

"I hope so," Brenda said. "We only have four days left."

Again, Jerry's stomach churned. In four days he was going to have to deliver a speech he hadn't even started writing. Tonight was the night; he *had* to write his opening remarks.

Ms. Robertson had come to this meeting to check out the progress of the plans for the fair. "Let's list the groups," she said and ticked them off on her fingers. "We've got a stage-fighting demonstration, someone to talk about Elizabethan clothes, a madrigal group to sing, jugglers, magicians, games out on the field, a replica of the Globe Theater with people to describe the Elizabethan theatrical experience, demonstrations of the dancing of that era—" She stared straight ahead. "Am I missing anything?"

"Josh will talk about jousting," Mr. Hooten said.

"That's right, jousting." Ms. R. smiled and gazed around the table. "The festival was a great idea. Thank you for thinking of it. I think our friends and families will be impressed with all your hard work.

And Jerry will start us all off with a welcoming speech." She smiled at him.

"Uh, yeah." His stomach wrenched for a third time.

"It might be a good idea in your speech, Jerry, to introduce all the demonstrations that are going on at the festival," she said. Jerry nodded, and Ms. R. smiled. "I'm sure it'll be wonderful. We've come to expect good things from you."

Jerry forced a smile. "Thanks."

He saw Gabe look up sharply toward Mr. Hooten's open door. He'd almost forgotten that Gabe was at the meeting. He'd seen him walk into the room at the beginning of sixth period, but he'd sat next to Elena and hadn't said a word.

Now Gabe scowled and made a shooing gesture with his hand, as if to tell whoever was in the hall to go away.

"Marshall!" the voice called in a loud stage whisper. "What're you doin' in there?"

Mr. Hooten looked up and called out. "Young man, come in here."

Craig's head and shoulders appeared in the doorway from around the corner. "Hunh?" Jerry thought he looked particularly goofy, with a big, surprised grin on his face.

"We're having a meeting in here," Mr. Hooten said. "Where are you supposed to be?"

"No place," he said. He met Jerry's eyes and his

grin widened. He disappeared again as he called out, "Hey, Flack, I'll be waiting to see you wearin' that *dress* at the festival!"

All eyes in the room focused on Jerry, who felt his face get hot and stingy.

"My locker partner," Jerry mumbled. "He thinks he's funny."

Mr. Hooten cleared his throat. "Well, it looks as if the festival's ready to go."

Jerry was glad that Mr. Hooten didn't ask him about Craig's comment. He wanted the event to bring in lots of money, so they could buy the computers for the cafeteria. And he wanted it to go well.

But mostly, he just wanted to get it over with.

Jerry stood at the front door and watched the last first grader climb into a car in the driveway.

"How's the play going?"

Jerry turned to see his dad standing behind him. His mouth was full, and he held a half-eaten apple.

"Okay," Jerry said. "Our dress rehearsal is tomorrow after school, and they'll present it in class the next day. I think they're about ready. I mean, the play isn't anything great, but they know their lines, and they've worked hard."

Melissa tore through the foyer from the living room, her spiky hair standing in stiff peaks on top of her head.

"We're gonna be so *great*," she announced over her shoulder as she disappeared up the stairs. "We're going to knock Mrs. Loonybin's socks off!"

The fragrance of mousse trailed after her.

"Any chance you can disabuse her of the practice of calling her teacher that unflattering name?" Mr. Flack asked.

"I doubt it," Jerry answered.

"How about convincing her that her hairstyle is unattractive?"

"No chance," Jerry answered. "But I know someone who can. And I'm going to call her right now."

His dad nodded. "Good luck," he said before taking another bite. With his cheeks stuffed with apple, looking rather like a chipmunk, he mumbled, "I don't know how much longer I can stand the sight of her looking so weird."

Jerry climbed the stairs, went to his room, and got the slip of paper with Zoey's phone number. In his parents' room, he settled on the floor and dialed. Zoey answered.

"Hey, Zoey. It's me, Jerry."

"Hey."

"I have another favor to ask."

"Okay."

"You think you could point out to my sister that she looks stupid with her hair standing up in spikes?"

Jerry heard the surprised smile in Zoey's voice.

"She's still wearing it like that?"

"Every day after school," Jerry answered. "She thinks it's cool. I think you know who convinced her of that."

"Geez, I was kidding."

"Well, she thinks you were serious. You want to come over tomorrow after school and let her know you didn't mean it?"

"Sure. See you tomorrow."

"Great. Oh, and Zoey?"

"Yeah?"

"How's Cinnamon doing?"

"Okay."

"Did you tell her the difference between cool and popular?" he asked.

"She's not ready for that."

"Oh." Jerry was itching to ask Zoey what she'd said to Cinnamon in the hallway. He waited a moment for Zoey to tell him.

She didn't.

He knew it wasn't any of his business. So he didn't ask.

"Well, thanks, Zoey," Jerry said finally. "My parents and I all thank you. We can smell Melissa coming a mile away."

"No problem. See you."

Jerry put down the phone. At least that was one less thing to complicate his life. He hoped.

* * *

Jerry sat at his desk in his room and stared at the blank computer monitor. He was waiting for ideas to present themselves for his welcoming speech, but they refused to come. Instead, they lurked just out of reach inside his head, sometimes leaping out, teasing him with a wave or a pirouette, then disappearing again around some dimly lit corner of his brain before he could focus on them.

He was having trouble concentrating. Even if all the other things in his life worked themselves out— the first graders' play and the social life of the students in his class—there was one awful problem left that he couldn't fix: getting the pup away from Craig.

In his mind's eye, he kept seeing the pup as she cowered at the tree in the park, barking as ferociously as her little voice could manage, while the geese attacked her from all sides.

Poor pup. Jerry wanted so badly to rescue her from Craig's neglect and give her to Brenda, who would love and care for her.

Craig's final words from the park came back to taunt Jerry. *"You're not gettin' her. Unless, of course, Flack, you wear a dress to that festival thing."* And then the latest taunt in front of the sixth-grade committee and Mr. Hooten and Ms. Robertson.

Craig had issued the challenge so many times that Jerry wondered if maybe he really *would* give up the pup if he gave his speech wearing a dress. Most of the kids at school knew about Craig's challenge.

The word had gotten around even faster than Craig's daring him to eat dog food. If Jerry were really stupid enough to wear a dress to the festival, and Craig didn't give him the pup, Craig would certainly lose face. And Craig would never want that to happen. His status at school was important to him.

But, of course, Jerry *wasn't* stupid enough to wear a dress. There was no way he would do that.

He sighed and hit the keys to get to his favorite search engine. He typed "Elizabethan times" in the subject box and found a long list of articles. One by one, he read the pieces, hoping something would nudge his brain with an idea for his speech.

It was the seventh article that caught his attention.

"Oh, yeah." Jerry's breathing quickened while he scanned the article. "How could I have forgotten? Maybe . . ."

He got up, hurried into his parents' room, and dialed Brenda's number.

"Brenda? Jerry. I think maybe I've figured out what I'm going to say in my speech. And wait till you hear this part—I'm going to try to get the pup for you. But you have to help me. Can you come over right now? I'm going to call Zoey, too. We'll need her help. We have a lot of work to do."

Jerry smiled and put down the receiver.

Maybe—just maybe—he could save the pup after all.

Chapter Sixteen

"Hi, Jerry."

He was waiting for Brenda at the oak in front of the school the next morning. As usual, the school grounds were crowded with students. Hearing his name, he turned to see Cinnamon O'Brien smile and twiddle her fingers. She walked over and planted herself in front of him.

Jerry realized that his mouth had dropped open, so he closed it. "Hey, Cinnamon."

He'd never seen Cinnamon looking more beautiful than she did today. She wore a kelly-green sweater with yellow and green butterfly clips in her hair. Her red hair, which had golden highlights in the sun, was once again curled and lustrous, falling over her shoulders in huge waves. But most of all, she looked happy, her dazzling blue eyes clear and smiling.

"What's up?" he asked her, hoping she couldn't tell that he'd been rattled by her beauty.

"Nothing." The way she smiled told him she could tell. "Just checking."

"On what?"

"On—oh, never mind."

Jerry was surprised that Cinnamon could have this effect on him. After all, he'd gotten over his crush on her about a month ago.

She gazed intensely into his eyes, the soft fragrance of her perfume caressing his senses, and he felt his breath leave him.

"Do you see him over there?" She was talking out of the corner of her mouth, her lips barely moving.

In a daze, Jerry started to turn. "Who?"

"Don't look now!" she said softly, but with a fierce edge.

"Oh." Startled, he turned back. "Where am I supposed to look?"

"At me for a sec." She didn't turn her head, but her eyes slid to the side. "Okay, now take a quick look to your left, as if you're just looking around normally, and see if he's there."

"Who?"

"Sandy—who do you think?"

"Oh. Sure."

Jerry glanced up to his left and back at her. "Yeah, he's there."

"Is he looking this way?"

"Yes."

Cinnamon threw her head back and laughed theatrically. But musically, he had to admit.

"Oh, good," she said, putting a hand on his arm and tilting her head in a cute pose. "I'm sooo glad."

She's been practicing in front of a mirror, he thought. She was certainly perfecting her insincere, phony self.

"I'm ignoring him, ya see," Cinnamon said in a low voice, still beaming that glorious smile at him.

"Sure." Jerry nodded and smiled a little. He didn't know what else to say in this pretend conversation.

"Well," Cinnamon said, "I guess I'll just walk away now."

"O-kay." Jerry didn't know how to act or where to look.

"Laugh, like we had a great talk," Cinnamon whispered, smiling.

"Ha-ha-ha!" Jerry laughed. He failed miserably to be convincing.

"Really rotten laugh, Jerry." Cinnamon's laugh was musical again, but loud, as she drifted off.

Oh, man, Jerry thought. That was one weird conversation.

Brenda arrived moments later. "Was that Cinnamon you were talking to? How's she doing?"

"Well, she looked happy. Zoey must've said something that worked."

"I hope so," Brenda said. She looked happy today, too, and full of hope. "Jerry, I'm so excited about your speech at the festival. I hope your idea works."

Jerry's stomach was suddenly full of butterflies. He put an arm around her shoulder and thought for a moment how nice it was that Brenda was always herself.

"I hope so, too, Bren."

Jerry went through the morning trying not to think about what he was going to do at the festival. It was daring, but he hoped he could pull it off.

"Remember, we have to get fitted for our costumes," Brenda reminded him just before lunch.

"Right," Jerry said. "The costume people are trying to get finished, and they're working during their lunch period. You want to go now? We can grab lunch afterward."

"Sure," Brenda said.

They walked down the hall toward the home and family classroom.

Brenda nudged Jerry. "Look at Elena; she looks so happy."

The tall sixth grader stood next to her locker,

smiling and talking with Gabe. She looked up and saw them and waved.

"Hey, Jerry," she called out. "You should see the stage combat class now. Everyone's doing a great job."

"Are you going to be demonstrating at the festival?" he asked.

"Yeah," she said. "Gabe and I, and several other partners, will be going through our paces."

"Great," he said, walking closer. "Oh, I have to introduce all the demonstrations, so I should talk to you about what I should say."

"Sure," Elena said. Jerry couldn't help but notice that she looked radiant. What was it about girls who were especially happy? Why did they look as if they were standing in spotlights? "We have practice right after school, but maybe afterward." She glanced at Gabe. "Gabe and I could show you what we're going to do."

Gabe nodded.

"That'd be good," Jerry said. "But I have to go home after school. Could you guys come over?"

"Sure."

"I know where you live," Gabe said. "We'll be there about four."

"Okay." Jerry figured his sister's play rehearsal wouldn't get started right away, so he could see the stage combat demonstration before it started. "See you."

Jerry and Brenda walked down the hall and turned the corner.

"Can you believe that Gabe Marshall's actually coming to my house," Jerry asked, "because I *invited* him?"

"About two weeks ago, I'd have said that was impossible."

"Elena's influence on him has been amazing."

They walked into the home and family classroom.

"Wow, look at all this," Brenda said.

The room was crowded with students, some trying on half-made garments, others pinning costumes together, still others sitting at sewing machines. Long tables were piled with patterns, fabrics, spools of thread, measuring tapes, and scissors.

"Hey, guys," Kim said, hurrying over. "I'm glad you're here. We need to get the costumes made."

She put her hands on her hips and scrutinized Jerry. "You need something special because you'll be up in front of everybody."

Jerry's heart *ka-blammed*, and he glanced at Brenda. "Could you give me something comfortable?"

"You should have something black," Kim said. "A natural black dye was hard to get in Elizabethan times, so black clothes were expensive and mostly worn by people with money. You'll look important in black."

Brenda asked, "What other colors were expensive?"

"Bright red was fashionable and hard to get," Kim said. "Blue was usually worn by servants, and poor people wore browns and grays." She looked again at Jerry. "Okay. First, we'll need to get you some tights."

Jerry rolled his eyes. "Great."

"And you should have Venetian breeches over those."

"What's that?"

"Trousers that come to your knees. I should be able to make those for you tonight and tomorrow."

"Okay."

"And a doublet. That's a short jacket. I'll need help with that."

"Is everyone wearing elaborate costumes like this?" Jerry asked. "How do you have time—"

"Nope," Kim said. "Only you and a few others. We're just suggesting the rest of the costumes. You know, tights and knee-length shorts. We're sewing a lot of loose shirts that'll work for smocks. And we have a few capes."

"What about me?" Brenda asked. "I don't need anything very fancy."

"Your mother have a long skirt?" Kim asked.

"I'll see."

"Maybe a peasant blouse with a shawl? That'd work."

"Okay. I know she has a peasant blouse."

"Good. I need to take some measurements on Jerry, and we'll get started on his costume."

"Hey, Jerry." Cinnamon rushed over. "I think Sandy's changing his mind about . . ." She lowered her voice to a whisper. "About, you know."

"Dumping you?" Kim asked.

"Kim!" Brenda cried.

"Oh." Kim frowned. "Sorry."

Cinnamon's face turned red. "He didn't dump me!"

"Really?" Kim asked. "Oh, sorry, I misunderstood. I thought everyone said he dropped you like a hot potato." She shrugged. "Must've been somebody else."

Cinnamon opened her mouth to protest, but Kim turned to Jerry. "I'll get a tape measure and be right back."

Cinnamon glared at Kim's back, her eyes narrow. "I don't like that girl," she said.

"She's harmless, Cinnamon," Brenda told her. "Really."

"So Sandy's changing his mind?" Jerry asked.

"Yeah." A sly smile formed on Cinnamon's lips. "I think he likes me again."

"That was fast," Jerry said. "What happened?"

"I think he just realized that he should be with a girl like me." She gazed at Jerry as if he should understand. "You know."

"I do?" Jerry asked.

"Yeah. A girl who's, well . . ." She glanced self-consciously at Brenda and back at Jerry. "A girl who matches him. You know. In cuteness."

"He's a man of substance then," Brenda said with a straight face.

"Exactly."

Jerry smiled. "That's great, Cinnamon."

"Oh. I hear that you'll need to know stuff about the costumes for your speech."

"Yeah, but not much."

"Well, I know everything you need to know," Cinnamon said. "Why don't I call you tonight?"

Jerry nodded. "That would be great. Talk to you later."

Jerry and Brenda gazed at his little sister, who was scurrying among the other first graders in the backyard, getting ready for their dress rehearsal. She wore blue jeans and a T-shirt that said, HONK IF YOU LOVE ROCK 'N' ROLL. Her hair, as usual, stood up in moist peaks all over her head.

"She's really going to wear her hair like that for the play?" Brenda asked.

"Not if Zoey gets here. She promised to come and tell Melissa it looks stupid."

"I hope she doesn't embarrass her," Brenda said. "Missy's just trying to be cool."

Jerry turned to see Zoey stroll into the yard.

"We'll know soon. Hey, Zoey. I'm glad you're here."

Zoey squinted over at Melissa's heavily moussed head, and a slight grin appeared on her lips. "Man, she really bought it."

"Yeah," Jerry said. "You have to be careful what you say to people. They seem to be willing to follow you, whatever you say or do."

Zoey nodded thoughtfully. "Cool."

"Well, not always," Jerry said. "Would you please talk to her?"

"Done." Zoey sauntered toward Melissa, who saw her and exclaimed, "Zoey!" and ran to greet her.

Be nice, Jerry told Zoey silently. She's just a kid.

Jerry and Brenda watched as the two huddled under the tree, Zoey talking softly and Melissa speaking occasionally, then listening and nodding.

"Okay," Melissa said after half a minute. She hurried over to Jerry. "Hey, can you wait a minute to start rehearsal? I need to wash my hair real fast."

Whoa. Melissa obviously wasn't hurt or embarrassed or anything.

"Sure," Jerry said. "We'll wait ten minutes. Then we have to start."

"Be right back," Melissa said, running toward the house.

"Man. Come on." Jerry and Brenda walked over to Zoey. "I don't know what you said, but it was perfect."

Zoey shrugged. "I asked her if she liked her hair that way."

"Yeah?"

"She admitted it was kind of sticky."

"Really?"

"I told her that very cool people do what *they* want and not what other people tell them is cool."

"So she really didn't like it in the first place?" Jerry asked.

"She may be six years old, but she's not stupid. She's also rather cool."

Jerry smiled. "Thanks, Zoey. By the way—I'm very curious about what you said to Cinnamon. She says Sandy likes her again."

Zoey shrugged. "Sandy likes pretty packages. I just suggested she doll herself up and ignore him."

Jerry laughed. "I guess it worked. You want to stay for the rehearsal?"

Zoey shrugged. "Sure," she said and drifted away toward the big tree.

Jerry watched her go. "Zoey strolls in, has a one-minute conversation, and changes a person completely." He shook his head in amazement. "She should teach seminars on this stuff."

Chapter Seventeen

"Jer-ry!"

Jerry turned to see Cinnamon and Sandy walking down the sidewalk, their arms around each other.

"They're really back together," Brenda whispered.

"I decided to come and give you the costume information in person," Cinnamon said.

And show us that you and Sandy are back together, he added to himself. Aloud, he said, "Hey, Sandy."

"Hey."

"What are all the little kids doing here?" Cinnamon asked.

"They have a dress rehearsal for a first-grade play," Jerry told her.

"Oh, I love plays! Let's stay, Sandy."

"Yeah, it could be funny," he answered.

"Well, okay, but be nice," Jerry said. "They've worked hard."

"Of *course* we'll be nice," Cinnamon said. "Where should we sit?"

"Over here on the grass," Jerry told her. "The stage is in front of the tree. We'll be starting in a few minutes."

Cinnamon and Sandy walked off to choose their spot.

Brenda grabbed Jerry's arm. "Uh-oh. Here come Elena and Gabe. You want me to head them off before Cinnamon and Sandy see them?"

"No," Jerry answered. "I think it'll be okay. Sandy seems to be happy with Cinnamon again."

"Hope so."

Elena and Gabe gazed over the yard at all the kids. "Are you baby-sitting?" Elena asked, smiling.

"No," Jerry said. "We're about to have a dress rehearsal of my sister's play."

"Sounds like fun," Elena said. "Can we stay and watch?"

"Uhhh." Jerry glanced over at Cinnamon and Sandy. "Did you see who else is here?"

"Sure," Elena said. She shrugged and looked at Gabe. "Do you mind?"

"I don't care," Gabe said.

Jerry wanted to say, *Gabe, you're so easy to get*

along with these days, but stopped himself. "Great," he said. "The kids could use the audience."

Cinnamon stood up from her seat in the grass, brushed off her jeans, and marched up to Jerry. "You didn't tell me *they* were going to be here," she said.

"Cinnamon," Elena said. "Let's sit together. I've been meaning to ask you how you get your hair to look so gorgeous."

Cinnamon opened her mouth, closed it, and opened it again like a fish. "Well, okay. Sure." She and Elena turned and walked, followed by Gabe, toward Sandy, who sat on the grass. "Of course, it's mostly natural," Jerry heard Cinnamon say, "but I could give you a few pointers."

He and Brenda grinned at each other. "Have a seat with the others," he said. "I'll hurry Melissa along. We've got a show to do."

Jerry made sure the first graders were ready to go, then he gave Melissa the sign to start, and sat next to Brenda.

Melissa stepped in front of the tree, cleared her throat, and spoke in a loud voice. "To Mrs. Loonybin—oh, I mean, Mrs. Loney and— Wait." She looked out over the sixth graders sitting in the audience, then plastered a big smile on her face. "I guess I mean, Hello, everyone!"

"Hello," Sandy called out from the audience and waved. Cinnamon waved, too.

Melissa looked surprised but pleased, and announced, "The curtain opens." She positioned herself a few steps back, and the first graders' play got under way.

Jerry had seen the play so often, he found himself watching the audience more than the actors.

When Melissa flitted onstage on her tiptoes, pretending to be Snowflake, the fairy who wanted to be human, everyone smiled, even Zoey. Elena turned to grin at Gabe, and she took his hand. Gabe looked happier than Jerry had ever seen him.

Jerry thought that Melissa played her part especially well that afternoon. As Snowflake, she spoke in a loud, clear voice, so everyone could hear her, even when a truck rumbled past on the street.

When the kids in the play said they loved burgers and fries, and Snowflake misunderstood and said, "Oh, I love burgers and flies, too," Cinnamon roared with laughter.

"Burgers and flies!" she repeated to Sandy. Sandy smiled and put his arm around her.

Snowflake proceeded to tell the kids lies about herself to convince them she was human.

Every time Jerry saw this scene, he couldn't help but think of the first few weeks of school when he told lies, so the students at school would think he was cool. He glanced over at Brenda, who was watching him with a little smile. She nodded and turned back to the first graders, and Jerry knew that she'd been reminded of the same thing. Good old Brenda, Jerry thought. He knew she'd never tease him about it.

Snowflake's lies to the kids at school came so often that she had trouble keeping track of them, and the kids began to figure out that she was very different.

One of the girls finally realized that she was a fairy, and she stole Snowflake's fairy dust. She threw it into her own face, and hollered, "I can fly! I can fly!" while she climbed the tree. She pretended to hover in midair over Snowflake and the other kids.

"Throw the dust over here," Sandy called out, clapping. "I want to fly, too." Everyone laughed.

"Me, too!" Cinnamon called out.

The other kids realized then that Snowflake was a fairy, not a girl, and they decided she was very cool because she had fairy dust and could fly any time she wanted to. The play ended with Snowflake giving a final monologue about how she'd decided to be herself. She could still be friends with the kids at school; they liked her for who she really was.

Except for Zoey, the sixth graders cheered as the young actors took their bows. Zoey smiled at Jerry.

"I wrote the whole thing!" Melissa announced proudly.

"No kidding," Gabe said and laughed. "I'd never have guessed."

The sixth graders stood up. Elena smiled at the girls. "You did a great job."

"Congratulations!" Brenda said.

"Very cool," Zoey added.

The first graders smiled.

Jerry sighed with relief. It was over, and the girls were finally ready to present their play for their class. One less thing to worry about.

Of course, one last thing was hanging over his head: the speech at the Elizabethan Festival.

He had to pull it off. His reputation as class president was hanging in the balance. And if he did it right, he'd get the pup from Craig and hand her over to Brenda for good, loving care.

That was if it all went perfectly.

And that was a lot to expect.

During the next two days, Jerry worked on his speech at night, and practiced with Brenda and Zoey every day after school. He wished he had more time to get ready, but at the same time, he wanted to get the festival—and all that went with it—behind him.

Friday morning, he walked into school with Brenda.

"He's already here," Jerry said. He nodded at Craig, who stood at their locker. Craig threw his jacket on the bottom of the locker on top of his other stuff and slammed the door shut.

"I'll come with you," Brenda said.

. They walked over and stopped in front of Craig.

"Hey, Craig," Jerry said.

Craig turned around. "Hey."

"I just wanted to tell you, you win."

"I win?" Craig looked puzzled.

"Yeah," Jerry said. "You win the challenge. Bring the pup to the festival tonight."

A slow, mean grin formed on Craig's face. "You gonna wear a *dress* during your speech? That's the only way you'll get her."

"Yeah, I'm going to wear a dress. But we want the pup right after my speech."

Craig hooted and said in a loud voice, *"You kiddin' me? You're really gonna wear a dress, Flack? What a sap! That's so cool!"*

Students in the hallway turned to look. Jerry could feel his face heating up.

"Ya hear that?" Craig hollered to anyone who might listen. "Come to the festival tonight, and see the sixth-grade president in a *dress*!" He laughed loudly. "Wait till I tell Gabe!"

"I'm glad you're happy, Craig," Jerry said. "But I don't walk onstage until you show me the pup."

"I'll have it there." He turned to Brenda and scowled. "*Her.* I'll have *her* there."

The school day moved slowly. Jerry had trouble concentrating on his classes; he kept watching the hands drag themselves around the face of the clock, as if they were heavily weighted. He checked his watch several times to make sure they hadn't stopped.

Of course, the news that he was going to wear a dress at the festival swept through the school like a windstorm.

"I just heard the wildest rumor about you, Flack!" a guy said between first and second periods.

"Jerry, tell me you're not *really* wearing a dress to the festival," said Scott after second hour. He had a pleading look on his face as if he was worried that if Jerry wore a dress, it would somehow humiliate every guy in school.

"Jerry Flack," said Aubrey Lane, "you're not really wearing a dress to get that puppy, are you? There *has* to be a less humiliating way."

Jerry just smiled a little and hurried on. What could he say? He couldn't lie and say he *wasn't* wearing a dress to the festival. But he didn't want to talk about it. Wearing the dress was going to be bad enough without having to discuss and explain it ahead of time.

At lunch, Kim and Kat Henley kept stealing glances at him. Kat finally blew out a big breath.

"Okay, Jerry, I can't take it anymore!" She turned to her sister. "I can't *not* say it!" She turned back to Jerry. "I'm so proud of you for agreeing to wear the dress to the festival. You're going to save that poor little dog, and all the laughter and jeering and booing, and all the disgusted, sarcastic comments will be worth it! You'll see."

Jerry felt himself shrink in his chair.

"But, Jerry," Kim said. "I worked so hard on that costume! I can't believe that you're not going to wear it."

"Oh, your hard work wasn't wasted," Jerry said. "Everyone will see it, I promise."

Tony and Chad glanced at each other. "Are you sure you want to do this?" Tony asked him. "Maybe you could challenge Craig to a wrestling match instead. I'll even wrestle him for the pup, if you want me to, since you're not really the wrestling type."

"Thanks, Tony," Jerry said, "but it'll be fine."

Tony looked at him, his voice heavy with pity. "Don't do it, Jerry."

Brenda spoke up. "Jerry has an idea. Wait and see. I think he can do it."

Jerry hoped she was right. If the crowd made fun and jeered and booed, it wouldn't work, and he'd be humiliated beyond belief. Ms. Robertson and his parents would be embarrassed for him, feel he'd let them down, and maybe never forgive him.

And he'd be forever known as *a midsummer night's dork.*

Chapter Eighteen

"Okay, I think we're all set," Jerry's mother said. The family was preparing to leave for the festival. She zipped her jacket and smiled at him. "Are you nervous, honey?"

"No."

What a lie. His insides were quivery, his hands were shaking, and he'd had to run to the bathroom three times in the last half hour.

Think of the pup; think of the pup; think of the pup, he repeated to himself. *That's why I'm doing it; that's why I'm doing it; that's why I'm doing it.*

"Interested to hear your speech," his dad said. "The first big speech of your presidency."

Whoo, boy.

"I bet it'll be bor-ing," Melissa said.

That's what you think, Jerry thought. He wondered if anyone would actually listen to the speech.

"What's in the bags?" his mother asked, on the way out to the car.

Jerry had stuffed the costume that Kat had made for him into two grocery sacks. But of course, he wasn't going to wear it.

"Uh, just some stuff I need to take to school."

In the parking lot at Hawthorne Middle School, Jerry leaped out of the car. "See you later." He closed the car door.

"Break a leg, honey," his mother said through the open window.

Jerry wondered if he really broke a leg before the speech was over, would his mother forgive him for wearing the dress? That scenario would, at least, have a sympathy factor.

He hustled into the school and made his way to the gym. Many of the sixth graders and their families were already there. Brenda was waiting for him just inside the gym door.

"Got it?" he asked her.

"Yes." She thrust a large bag at him. "There's a safety pin in the bottom in case the skirt's waistline is too big."

"Thanks. Here's yours." Jerry handed her the two bags with the costume Kat had made.

"See the platform at the far end of the gym?" Brenda asked. It looked like a small stage with a microphone. "You'll be giving your speech there."

"Okay." Jerry blew out a nervous breath. "Craig had better bring the little dog tonight."

"Oh, he *has* to!" Brenda cried. "That's what all our work was for!"

"Let's go change. Meet you here in a couple of minutes."

"Right."

They split up to go to their own bathrooms. Jerry pushed in the door to the men's room and walked into a stall at the far end. He closed the door and locked it.

He opened the sack, took out the blouse, and held it up. It had puffy sleeves and gathers around the neckline.

Oh, man. Did he really have to wear this thing?

Yes, he had to. If he wanted to get the pup away from Craig.

He took off his sweatshirt and hung it on the hook. He put on the blouse. *Ick.* It felt as bad as it must look.

He blew out a breath. *Think of the pup; think of the pup.*

He took off his shoes and then his jeans and hung the jeans over the sweatshirt on the hook.

He froze. The bathroom door had just opened,

and someone walked in.

Make it fast, he ordered silently, hardly daring to breathe.

He heard the appropriate noises, and after a minute, the footsteps shuffling out of the bathroom.

He started breathing again. He took a pair of denim shorts out of the bag and put them on, then took out the skirt and put it on over the shorts. The waistline of the skirt was bigger than he needed, so he pinned it closed with Brenda's safety pin. The sweatshirt and jeans he shoved into the bag, but he moved the wig to the top of the pile inside the bag.

The wig. *Oh, geez.* He left it inside the bag.

Jerry put on his shoes, and then the jacket he'd brought with him, and he bunched the skirt up over his waist, tucking some of it into his denim shorts. The rest, he stuffed up inside his jacket. He'd have to be sure the skirt didn't show below the edge of his jacket.

He took a big, shaky breath and wiped his damp palms on his jean shorts.

Here goes.

He picked up the bag and walked out of the bathroom, keeping his arms pressed to his sides to keep the skirt above his waist. He spotted Brenda just inside the gym; she was wearing the tights, breeches, and doublet.

"Hey."

She turned and looked him up and down. "Where's the skirt?"

"Inside the jacket."

Brenda nodded. "It's cotton, so it'll be very wrinkled when you let it down. But I don't blame you for keeping it hidden until you have to give the speech."

"Let's look around and see if we can spot Craig," Jerry said. "I'm not going through with this if he doesn't show up."

"What'll you do instead?"

Jerry thought a second. "I guess I'll wing it."

Ms. Robertson appeared at his side. "There you are, Jerry. Looks as if we have a good turnout tonight." She looked at Brenda's costume. "Brenda, why are you wearing a man's—"

"It's a surprise," Brenda said.

Ms. R. frowned. "A surprise?"

"Yes."

She looked doubtful. "Well, I don't know . . ."

"Trust us," Brenda said.

"Okay," Ms. R. said. She smiled. "I don't know what you two have up your sleeves, but I'm sure it'll be fine. You've never let me down yet."

Something wilted inside of Jerry, but he forced a smile. "I hope you like it."

"Are you about ready to give your welcoming speech?"

"Well . . ." He glanced nervously at Brenda. "Yes,

but in a few minutes, okay?"

Ms. R. checked her watch. "We should start pretty soon, so we can get the demonstrations going."

"Be just a few minutes."

"Good." She left.

"Come on," Jerry said. "Let's look for Craig."

"Maybe he's outside. Maybe someone told him he couldn't bring the puppy into the school."

"Let's look."

They strode out of the gym, down the hallway, and out the school door.

"I'll walk around by the athletic field, and you look on the street side, okay?"

"Right," said Brenda.

Jerry walked around the entire school, but he didn't see Craig or the pup. He met Brenda back at the side entrance.

"Maybe you'd better think of a plan B," Brenda said. "What if Craig wants to keep the puppy?" Worry was creasing a vertical line between her eyebrows.

"Who knows?" Jerry said.

A small part of him felt relief. Maybe he wouldn't have to give the speech he'd planned wearing the skirt. But he gazed into Brenda's eyes and saw the results of nearly two weeks of frustration, disappointment, and sadness. She'd fallen in love with the pup that first day they'd seen her flying down the street on the loose. Brenda had wanted so much to give her a good home.

Tears formed in her eyes. "I'm just afraid Craig will go back on his word again."

"I know. I'm sorry."

Jerry put his arms around her, and she rested her head on his shoulder. While he stroked her hair, he started putting together a new welcoming speech in his head.

Welcome, everyone, to the Hawthorne sixth-grade Elizabethan Festival. We've been working hard these last two—

"Jerry, Ms. Robertson has been looking for you!" It was Kat who was speaking; she was also jabbing him hard on the shoulder. "You have to give your speech now! Hurry up!"

"I'm coming." Brenda pulled away, and he looked at her carefully. "You okay?"

Brenda sniffed. "Yeah. Come on."

Jerry, Brenda, and Kat walked back into the school and to the gym.

"Brenda's wearing the costume?" Kat asked, looking her up and down. "It's actually kind of cute on you."

"Thanks."

Craig stood inside the gym door. He wore a bulky jacket.

"Craig!" Brenda shouted.

"Where's the dog?" Jerry asked. "Didn't you bring her?"

Craig unzipped his jacket, and a little black-and-white head popped out.

"Oh, puppy!" Brenda cried out. She reached for the pup, but Craig pushed her away. "You're not wearin' a dress, Flack."

Jerry took off his jacket and let the wrinkled cotton skirt fall to his ankles, covering his denim shorts. He reached into the bag, pulled out the wig with long, blond curls, and jammed it onto his head.

"The wig's backward, Jerry." Brenda rotated it on his head. "There."

Jerry stood there before Kat, Brenda, Craig, and the whole gym full of people, dressed in the white peasant blouse, skirt, and wig. He'd forgotten about wearing something appropriate on his feet, so his athletic shoes stuck out from under the skirt. Jerry felt dozens of eyes on him, and his face heated up so fiercely, he could feel his pulse in his cheeks.

Jerry pushed his face up close to Craig's. "There. You see me? I'm wearing a dress. That's my part of the bargain."

Craig hooted loudly. "Our president Jerry Flack's wearin' a *dress*! Looks real attractive on you, Flack! Hey, Marshall!" He waved his arm over his head. "Get over here and see this!" He lowered his voice. "But you have to give your speech dressed like that."

Gabe strolled over, frowning at Jerry.

Jerry said to Gabe, "You know the bargain I have

with Craig, right? That I give the speech in a dress, and he turns over the pup to Brenda and me."

"Yeah," Gabe said. He scratched his cheek and gave Jerry a doubtful look.

"You stay here with Craig and the pup, will you?" Jerry asked him.

"Okay."

"I want to make sure Craig delivers the pup after the speech." Jerry said to Brenda, "Let's go."

They strode across the gym floor toward the platform. Jerry tried to look straight ahead, but he caught sight of Ms. R.'s face as he hurried past. Her mouth dropped open. "Jerry! What are you doing?"

But he kept walking. He couldn't stop now.

"Look at Flack! He's wearing the dress!" someone said.

"That's not a dress; it's a skirt," one girl said. "And a wig. Is that the dorkiest thing you've ever seen, or what?"

His parents turned to see him, and he saw the look of horror on their faces.

"Jerald Evan Flack!" he heard his mother cry over the murmurs around him.

"Mom, is that *Jerry*?" Melissa asked. "Yuck."

This has to work; it has to.

Jerry and Brenda approached the platform, and Jerry set the bag on the floor and stepped up to the microphone. A guy with a camera stepped forward and took some pictures, while a woman standing next to him scribbled in a notebook.

A hush fell over the gym, and the crowd moved closer. He began his speech.

> *"We do not wish to offend today*
> *but to demonstrate right here the way*
> *that actors worked in Shakespeare's time*
> *where boys played girls, and that's why I'm*
> *dressed in these clothes to welcome you.*
> *We invite you to walk around and view—"*

Jerry saw understanding and amusement come into Ms. R.'s face. His parents visibly relaxed, too. Some of the sixth graders were grinning.

> *"the demonstrations we have planned.*
> *Your every wish is our command.*
> *So if you wish to see a fight*
> *you'll watch stage combat to your right.*
> *Or if in fact you'd rather know*
> *how William Shakespeare put on a show*
> *a model of the Globe is here.*
> *Students there will make it clear*
> *where actors stood to say their lines*
> *and people, rich and poor—all kinds—*
> *came to see the plays. And you*
> *can see how common clothes looked, too.*
> *We have singers, jugglers, and magic.*
> *To miss any of them would be tragic.*

On the field are games to play,
and so we hope you'll plan to stay.
But first, we'd like for you to see
a scene that we wrote recently.
Inspired by A Midsummer Night's Dream,
Imagine us under glow of moonbeam.
A forest's where the scene takes place
and to remind, so I won't lose face—
remember that in Shakespeare's time
a woman onstage was thought a crime.
The part here that I will play,
is a girl's, so don't you go away.
I'll start it now if you'll agree
that Helena is who I'll be."

Jerry reached out to Brenda, who handed him a shawl. He put it around his shoulders, and whoops went up from a few students in the crowd. Then a few wolf whistles.

Jerry waited, and after some snickers, the gym became quiet again. He cleared his throat, then spoke in a light voice—not a falsetto, but pitched slightly higher than his own, with more breath.

"O Demetrius, I am sick when I look not on you."

Laughter and groans were heard around the gym.

"It is not night when I do see your face."

Zoey, dressed in a man's costume, stepped out of the crowd and became Lysander. She said in a loud voice:

"Run through fire, I will, for thy sweet sake!"

Whoops went up from the crowd.

Then Brenda, wearing the Elizabethan man's clothing, entered and shouted her lines at Zoey:

"Out of my sight, Lysander!
I had a major crush on Helena before this.
And I've decided I like her again!
Do as you will to win her heart.
I'll stay by her side, till I make her mine!"

Several students in the audience whooped.

Zoey, as Lysander, cried:

"'Tis you, Demetrius! You swine! You cur!
Helena will pledge her love for me.
If you love her, put up your fists."

Jerry, keeping his voice light for Helena, said into the microphone:

"Boys, boys! Art thou kidding?"

His head tipped down, he looked out from under the blond curls of the wig and said:

"You want to fight over moi?*"*

More laughter and a few more wolf whistles were heard from the audience.

Brenda bowed low to Jerry and said:

"Allow me to defend your honor, sweet Helena."

Zoey cried:

"Fair Helena is sweet, but she's sweet on me!*"*

She lunged at Brenda and pushed her hard to the floor. Brenda lifted her foot to shove Zoey, but Zoey grabbed her foot and threw her backward onto the floor a few yards away.

Jerry cried out:

"You leave my Demetrius be!"

And he leaped off the stage, tripping slightly on his skirt. He recovered, took off his shawl and tossed it into the crowd. He hauled Zoey up from the floor, and swung his fist in a roundhouse punch toward Zoey's chin. A *smack* was heard. Zoey's head snapped to the side, and she staggered backward and fell.

A whoop went up from somewhere in the room. *"Get 'im, Helena!"* someone hollered.

More camera flashes were going off around Jerry.

Jerry turned away from Zoey, brushed his hands together, and said:

"That should discourage his love for me."

Zoey scrambled to her feet and said in a big man's voice:

"I had no idea you were so daring, my fair Helena."

Jerry smiled and said modestly:

"It was nothing."

Zoey crept up behind Jerry and grabbed him in a headlock. Jerry lunged forward and threw her over his shoulder onto the floor. She scrambled to her feet and rushed back at Jerry, and they traded blows, rolling around on the floor.

Brenda rushed toward the crowd where Elena stood. Brenda grabbed her and asked in a loud voice:

"Fair maid, have you a looking glass?"

Elena beamed and answered:

"Why yes, kind sir. And it's right here!"

She opened a bag and pulled out an oversized mirror and handed it to Brenda with a flourish.

"Thank you!"

Jerry and Zoey were still punching each other in the face and in the stomach. Jerry's skirt flew up, exposing his denim shorts, and people in the crowd laughed.

Brenda rushed over and crashed the big mirror into Zoey's head. The "mirror" shattered into thousands of tiny pieces; they tinkled as they hit the floor.

Zoey rolled her eyes back in her head and fainted in a dramatic swoon onto the floor.

Jerry picked himself up. A trickle of red blood ran down his chin and dribbled onto the peasant blouse. He grinned and cried out:

"Oh, Demetrius! You saved me!"

He picked Brenda up and carried her off toward the gym door, his skirt swinging.

He paused at the door, turned and waved to the crowd, and said, "Have a good time, everybody!" And he carried Brenda out the door while people laughed and applauded.

Chapter Nineteen

Jerry set Brenda on the floor outside the gym door as relief swept over him. It was finally over. The whole dress thing worked!

"Come on," he said, whipping the wig off his head. He took the safety pin off the skirt, stepped out of it, and threw it over one shoulder. Then he stuffed half the wig into the waistband of his denim shorts. "Let's go get the pup."

He and Brenda hurried back into the gym and stopped where they'd left Craig and Gabe.

"Where are they?" Jerry threw up his hands. "They were supposed to wait right here!"

The crowd had broken up and people were

scattering across the gym to watch the various demonstrations. Jerry and Brenda scanned the nearby faces, but they couldn't see either of the boys.

"You guys did a great job!" said Aubrey Lane, patting Jerry on the back.

"Thanks."

"Yeah," said Scott Perkins, who came up behind him. "That was awesome."

"Not to mention gutsy," added Aubrey. "Jerry, I don't know one other boy who would dress like a girl in front of the whole class!"

Scott grinned. "I sure wouldn't. You pulled it off, though."

Aubrey and Scott left, and Jerry and Brenda walked back to the gym door and stopped in front of it.

"Do you think Gabe let Craig leave with the puppy?" Brenda asked, her voice higher than usual. She looked around anxiously.

Elena rushed out of the crowd. "Have you seen Gabe? We need to start the stage fighting demonstration."

"We're looking for him, too," Jerry said.

"There he is!" Brenda pointed.

Jerry turned to look. Outside the gym door, through the windows, they saw Gabe hauling Craig toward them, dragging him by his arm. Jerry opened the door.

Craig was protesting and struggling to get away.

Gabe spotted Jerry and shoved Craig through the door.

"What's going on?" Jerry asked, letting the door swing shut.

"He was going to leave with the dog," Gabe said.

The puppy's head popped out of Craig's jacket again. Brenda cried out and positioned herself between Craig and the gym door, as if to stop him if he tried to get away. "Okay. Jerry did everything you wanted him to do. So the puppy is ours."

"You cheated," Craig growled.

"What!" Jerry scowled. "I did exactly what you said."

"It wasn't a *dress,*" Craig said. "It was a *skirt.* And you pretended you were an actor—and—and—"

"And nothing, Craig Fox!" Elena stepped forward, and Craig gazed up at her. She towered over him, and she set her fists on her hips, which added strength to her powerful presence. "You challenged Jerry, and he met your challenge. So hand over the pup."

Craig glared up at Elena, then appealed to Gabe. "He cheated."

Gabe rolled his eyes. "Hand over the dog, Fox."

"But—"

"Hand him over," Gabe repeated. "Jerry did his part."

"Just because you like *her,*" Craig snarled, glaring at Elena again.

But he unzipped his jacket, and Brenda scooped up the puppy from his arms. She laughed, and her laugh was filled with relief and joy.

"Oh, you sweet thing," she said. "You're so skinny, but we're going to go home, and I'm going to give you the best dinner you ever had."

The pup licked her face and wagged her whole backside. Craig walked off in a huff.

"Gabe, we have to start," Elena said.

"Right."

Elena handed Jerry his bag. "This is your stuff. Oh, Jerry. My aunt—the reporter? She's really impressed with you. She's writing a story about the festival, and a photographer was here, too, taking pictures. You guys were sooo good up there!"

Jerry smiled. "Thanks."

"You did a great job making that fake mirror," she said. "What was the 'glass' made of?"

"Sugar," Jerry said. "Just melted sugar."

"And the fake blood?"

"Mostly peanut butter and white corn syrup. And a little soap and food color." He grinned.

"It looked so real!" Elena laughed. She turned to Gabe. "Let's hope our stage combat looks as convincing."

"Good luck, you guys," Jerry called out.

"Thanks for your help, Elena," Brenda said. She hugged the puppy close. "Maybe we should take her outside."

They walked out the gym door and down the hall. The place was mostly deserted. Brenda touched Jerry's arm and they stopped in the middle of the corridor. She reached over and touched his face. "Jerry Flack, you're the very best friend I've ever had in my life. Nobody else would've done what you did to get me my little pup."

Jerry grinned. "Well, I can't think of anyone else I'd put on a dress for, that's for sure."

Brenda leaned in and kissed him over the puppy's head. "You know what I think I'll name her?"

"Pooch?" Jerry asked. He kissed her back.

She slapped him playfully on the arm. "Of course not!" she said, laughing. "I'm sort of going to name her after you."

"After me?"

"Sort of. I thought I'd name her Jeraldine. With a *J*."

"You sure you want to stick her with that name?"

"I wouldn't have her if you weren't my friend."

"But, Brenda. *Jeraldine?*"

"I love it. And you're not so bad yourself, Flack." She reached up and ruffled his hair. "Your hair's really growing."

"Come on," Jerry said. "Let's take Jeraldine for a walk."

Brenda laughed. "Well, maybe you should change your shirt first."

Jerry looked down. He was still wearing the peasant blouse. "Oh. Wait right here."

"Hey, Flack," Brenda said. "I'm not going anywhere unless you're there."

Jerry grinned. "Thanks, Bren," he said. "I'll be right back."

He turned and headed back toward the gym wearing a big grin on his face.